A Little Christmas: Matty Secret!

Daddy/Boy Gay Romance

JP Sayle

JP SAYLE

Book Cover © 2023 Wendy Rathbone

Editing Lucas Cornelius

Proofread by Virginie Toulon

Book Formatting by JP Sayle

References to real people, events, organisations, locations, or establishments are only intended to give a sense of authenticity and have been used fictitiously.

The author acknowledges the copyrighted or trademarked status and trademark of any goods.

Films, music, and lyrics mentioned are the property of the copyright holders.

Trigger Warnings:

Some of the content of this book contains sexually graphic scenes, with the use of explicit language, adult situations, and violence.

Story Outline

C *an a visit to a secret garden in Chicago give two men what they have been seeking—a relationship that fulfills both their needs?*

Finding a job after his discharge from the army proves an easy task for Weston Forrester.

Finding a 'boy'? Yeah, not so much. Until he meets Matty, who is all kinds of sweet, but needs time.

So Weston keeps it light, waiting for Matty to trust him.

Matty Bevan is a magnet for cheaters and liars, and Weston seems too good to be true, even if he does give off 'Daddy' vibes. But each encounter draws Matty closer. His heart on the line, he asks his best friend for help. Only things don't quite go according to plan.

A cute little fox is about to get his Christmas wish—except it's more than he bargained for.

A Little Christmas! Matty's Secret is part of A Little Christmas: Season Two 2023 multi-author series with themes loosely based on the classic book A Secret Garden. Each book in A Little Christmas is a standalone. But each boy is silly, unique, lovable, and downright adorable, so why not read them all.

Contents

Prologue

Matty

August

The weather was beautiful, warm without trying to sear the skin from my bones, so I'd dressed accordingly. My need to feel good was satisfied by an orange, ruffled sleeved top with white edging. If I squinted and tilted my head to the left, it kind of resembled the coloring of foxes, which I loved. My shorts were cream and the whole ensemble was finished off with a pair of Converse with foxes on them.

I spritzed my new fragrance in the air above my blond curls and waited for the scent to settle on my clothes before going to my bed. I'd laid out everything I wanted to take with me for my planned day out.

I slipped my fox ears inside the tiny backpack Austin, my best friend Gaines' Daddy, had bought me after a visit to the zoo. It was decorated with the faces of the bat eared baby foxes I'd seen and gushed over.

In the Daddy stakes, Gaines had won the lottery, not that our new friend Terrence hadn't as well. He had a wonderful Daddy who let us go over and play with Terrence in his playroom. My mood dipped as I thought about how my hopes of developing something with a guy recently had withered and died. He seemed nice enough, but I'd found out the creep had been lying about why he couldn't take me back to his apartment.

Creep number seven—yes, I had started to number them to keep them straight rather than give them names—failed to mention he already lived with a pet. A-hole pretended to like the fox persona my Little occasionally manifested as, when he actually preferred a pup. The fact he had a pup at home and just wanted to get his end away with me was why I never saw his place.

A sigh of relief was easier than getting all het up about something that was happening on a far too regular basis for my liking. At least I'd just escaped with a bruised ego this time.

"Where're you off to?" Gaines popped through my open door, a sunny smile lighting his beautiful face. "I was just coming to see if you wanted to go out with me and Daddy. We're going to the movies to watch the remake of Little Mermaid."

As tempting as it was, I was still licking my wounded pride at getting tricked by yet another creep and hadn't had the courage to tell Gaines about it when he was so happy. I loved my friend with all of my heart, but sharing that I was a loser magnet of epic proportions was getting more than a little embarrassing.

I amped up my smile. "Thanks, but I've got plans." It was the truth. I was off to explore another of Chicago's secret gardens. I'd been a little obsessed with the idea there were hidden gardens after watching the movie *The Secret Garden,* so I'd downloaded the book to my kindle. I had snacks and juice in my backpack to head out and find the next secret garden on my list. Then spend some time exploring before waiting for someone to find me... or not.

"Oh... if you're sure." The droop of Gaines' shoulders revealed his disappointment, even when the smile remained in place.

Picking up my pack, I slung it over my shoulders as I walked over to him, enjoying the waft of the new fragrance I'd bought, which claimed to be summer in a bottle. I slipped an arm around his waist and rested my head on his slim shoulder. "We could have some playtime later, when I get back?"

He kissed my cheek. "Great. I'll get Daddy to set up the play area downstairs. He's found some new koala toys and games for us to play with."

"You're so spoiled," I said, loving how he bounced with excitement next to me. He was wearing sweats because he'd taught an early morning pole dance class.

"Daddy spoils you, too," he pointed out as we walked down the stairs.

"Hey, I'm your best friend. He needs to keep me sweet."

Giggles erupted from Gaines and brought Austin from the direction of the kitchen. His weekend attire comprised of cargo shorts and a short sleeve button down, instead of the suit he wore for work.

"Did I hear my name being used in vain?" he growled, looking intimidating until anyone looked at his eyes, which held a world of love that was all aimed at Gaines.

An ache developed in the center of my chest at how I wanted what my friend had. I was grateful for Austin being the man he was, who understood that Gaines and I had a special friendship bond and hadn't tried to push me out. I'd lived with Gaines for years before he started dating Austin and he'd not, at any point, suggested I was cramping their style by staying. He was a good man and a perfect Daddy who only wanted Gaines to be happy.

"I think that's my cue to leave." I waved a hand at both of them and was out the door before the kissing started.

The sky was clear and bright with a hot ball of yellow that warmed my pale skin. I walked a little way from the house in West Montrose before checking out the closest Lyft to take me to the Milton Lee Olive park.

The ride didn't take long as the park was less than nine miles from my home. My driver was chatty, but not OTT, so when we stopped at the curb, I went into the app to give him a tip as I exited the car.

Happy I'd done the guy a solid, I clutched the straps of my pack and lifted my face, enjoying the light breeze coming off Lake Michigan. From what I'd read about the park, the place was a wedding photographer's dream and I hoped I might get to see a couple all dressed in their finery having their pictures taken.

I giggled at how finding a wedding party here wouldn't give me the secret garden vibe that I was after. The illusion I wanted was to be the only one who'd found this breathtaking and quiet Milton Lee Olive Park. I ambled down the tree-lined path that led to the water. The trees met above my head, forming an archway above me. If I shut my eyes I could almost imagine myself walking down to meet my Daddy on our wedding day.

You have to find a Daddy who isn't a cheater first!

Not wishing to let the snippy voice spoil my day, I blocked it quick-smart as I hummed to myself and continued on, inhaling the smell of summer. Flowers, heat, grass, and something sweet coming from somewhere that suggested there was a food vendor selling doughnuts. Thankfully, I couldn't see the vendor and give in to have one for a mid-morning snack.

Off to the side were Navy Pier and Oak Street Beach. The waterfront park had a perfect, unobstructed view of Lake Michigan and the towers that line Lake Shore Drive. Tall, scraggly honey locust trees framed the peaceful walking path along the lakefront and with no one around, it was everything I'd hoped it would be.

It was easy to believe I was alone and hidden from the world as I found a spot under a tree near the waters' edge and sat down on the grass, uncaring I might get a stain on my shorts. I leaned back against the solid tree after slipping off my pack. Laying it on the ground next to me, I rooted around inside to pull out my sunnies and slipped them on. Taking out my juice bottle with a sippy lid, I placed it next to my leg and laid out my snack box next to it. Finally, kindle in hand, I reached for my fox ears, slipping them on.

A sigh of contentment drifted past my lips at the peacefulness that was only occasionally broken by the cries of the gulls and the sound of water lapping gently against the shoreline.

Perfect.

For a moment, I shut my eyes, resting the kindle in my lap and letting myself find the right headspace to be Little. Outside, in public, it could be somewhat harder. Ideally, I'd have loved to have a Daddy come and read my book to me and let me rest my head on their lap.

You aren't helping with thoughts like that! If my Little side had a voice, it was surely the one griping in my head right then.

"Stop grumping at me, I'm trying," I muttered aloud.

"Are you okay?" A deep, gentle voice asked, startling me into opening my eyes.

My gaze traveled a very long way up a muscular body that looked like that of an athlete dressed in running shorts and a vest that was damp with sweat. Honey colored skin glistened as the gray-haired, blue-eyed hottie crouched down at the side of me, offering a smile that made me feel like I was the one who'd gone jogging, not him.

His bunching thigh muscles drew my attention to the hair covering his legs. Unlike the gray of his facial hair, or the thick hair atop his head, his leg hairs were a golden color that made me want to fan myself. Or reach out and touch to see if they were as silky soft as they appeared.

"Pumpkin, can you tell me if you're okay?"

He called me pumpkin... *he called me pumpkin!*

More heat crept up my body, reaching my cheeks in a second flat, and I offered a shy smile, unsure what else to do when his behavior screamed 'I'm a caring Daddy'.

"Yeah, sorry. I was talking to myself... though it's nothing to worry about. I do it from time to time." I was waffling, and I appeared unable to stop as I carried on. "It's just that sometimes it's the only way to make myself listen to reason."

Shut up, please!

His laughter was melodic and captivating and he didn't look at me like I needed to go and seek medical help. There was absolutely nothing condescending about it. I'd learned to tell the difference, just not how to spot a cheater or liar.

"Sometimes it's the only way to get a sensible answer. Or that's what Mom always told me when I found her talking to herself in the kitchen. Although, this was usually after Dad had left her and probably hadn't done what she wanted." The guy's smile was encouraging and totally not the kind that was trying to placate me.

That he was trying to make me feel better about being caught talking aloud made my smile widen. "Yeah, Mom does the same with Dad, only normally he's not left the room."

More laughter made my stomach bounce and came with a heavy dose of lust. No... *stop that right now!*

"I've promised myself that when I find a boy—friend, I'll learn from my parents' mistakes and listen to what my partner wants," he said.

I frowned.

He's single!

Was he hitting on me?

Did he stress the 'boy' part?

He rose, a gorgeous smile revealing straight, white teeth as he nodded to where I'd laid out my little picnic. "I can see you've set up a little's picnic, and I've interrupted your quiet."

When he glanced away, my head latched onto his phrasing once more. Little's. Was he meaning what I thought he was? Or was I just that desperate and seeing him as a Daddy?

I followed his gaze, finding that easier to do than think about how I could get myself into a whole heap of bother by misinterpreting what the hottie meant. How could someone like him be single? He was probably a player and just chancing his luck, as we were the only two people in sight.

Despite this, I realized I didn't feel the need to grab my pack and pull out my pepper spray. I decided keeping my thoughts to myself was probably best. Then I could daydream about the guy once he'd gone and pretend he was single and not a player. After all, the likelihood of seeing him again in a city the size of Chicago was slim to none.

"This is, as I remember, a perfectly kept secret garden to come and enjoy the quiet," he murmured, just loud enough for me to hear.

My heart jumped against my ribcage hard enough I lost the ability to suck in a breath at the meaning behind his words and the beautiful smile he aimed at me. For a moment, I wished I'd taken off my sunnies as he stared at me, not liking that he couldn't see me properly.

"Sorry for spoiling your alone time. Enjoy the rest of your day." Before I could say anything more, he gave me a kind of salute and jogged away, his ass flexing in the shorts as he disappeared in the direction I'd come from.

I blew out my breath and waved a hand in front of my overheated face.

"Wow," I said aloud. A player or not, he was still hot!

Chapter One

Weston

One Month Later

"What's it been Weston, five years? When did you get back to Chicago? And I'm sorry to hear about your dad," Austin said as he directed me to the chair opposite him.

A stab of grief came at how I'd missed my father's funeral. Fuck, I'd not known he'd died until two months after the fact. I had left my mom to cope alone and that, to me, was unforgivable. It had become a reality check of where my life was headed, and I'd spent a year rectifying that situation.

Part of that was reaching out to Austin when I'd heard he'd started his own business as I was in the market for a job. Financially, I was doing okay and didn't need to work full time, but I needed something to keep me occupied and stop me going out of my mind with boredom. Down time for more than a week or two left me pulling my hair out. A month being home and I was ready to crawl the walls.

Mom had encouraged me to find something to keep me busy after fixing everything in the family home and to stop the boredom—what she actually meant was getting under her feet. There was no one for me to go home to and spend all this additional time with. My career had been my focus to the detriment of everything else. I wanted—no, needed—to change that.

I sank into the leather chair, unbuttoning my suit jacket, and gave Austin a wide grin. "Thank you. It's been hard accepting he's gone. I've only just started to mourn his loss as I never got that closure of a funeral, of seeing him before..." I licked my drying lips, giving myself a second. "The old coot never told me how terrible things were. He'd sworn Mom to secrecy."

Austin came forward in his seat with a look of empathy. "That's gotta be tough. I liked your dad. He was a good man."

"He was. That doesn't mean I don't want to kick his ass for not giving me a chance to be there for him, for Mom."

Austin reached forward and placed a hand on my knee and squeezed. "I'm here if you ever wanna talk or get drunk."

I knew he wasn't the type to use alcohol to relieve his tension, but nodded at the offer to talk. "Thanks."

I pinched the bridge of my nose to quell the sudden ache in my eyes that often came from any talk about my old man. "Anyway, let's talk about you."

I dropped my hand and glanced about the office, which was on the top floor of the large house Austin had guided me through when I'd arrived. "Looks like business is good and that you might need another employee?"

His chuckle was rich and full-bodied. "Yes, and yes." He winked at me. "This is the reason you're here. As I said on the phone, we are drowning in the number of requests now word is fully out about what we offer. You tick all the boxes of what we are looking for in an employee."

I tugged on my trimmed beard, that had more gray than when we'd last seen each other. "I look in the mirror and I see an old graying man. You, on the other hand, don't look to have aged at all. So are you sure I'm what you're looking for?" I asked, only partly joking.

He snorted, and his gaze swept over me. "I think you're looking in a distorted mirror. If you're what old looks like, then I'm sure there are many that would sign up! I bet there's a fucking eight pack under that button-down."

My head shake came with laughter. "I can assure you it's not what it once was. My body doesn't like the punishment I used to give it." A hint of heat crept up my neck, past the collar of my button-down at how Austin's gaze appraised me. I'd once been known as 'Beast' in the gym. I was a tad competitive.

"Can you still do the trick with the ball while hanging from the bars? Man, you have no idea how pissed half the guys were at seeing you do that little trick."

Brows arching, I laughed, rocking in my creaking seat. "They never put in the effort. Liam always taught us that we had to be a hundred percent committed to achieve our goals." Liam was our old commander and a hard taskmaster.

Another snort and the hand he'd removed from my knee got pointed at me. "Liam was damn hard to please. And everyone did put in the effort." His eyes gleamed with amusement. "It was just your hand eye—or foot eye coordination was better than anyone else's!" he exclaimed.

I waved a hand at him. "Some of us are just more talented than others."

"Is that so?" His eyes narrowed. "You up for a little challenge?"

Intrigued, more than I suspected was good for me, when Austin looked far too smug, I shrugged nonchalantly. "Fine. But what will the wager be?"

The gleam never left Austin's eyes. "Do you have something in mind?"

My mind raced for something that would wipe the smirk off Austin's handsome face, even though he was an excellent friend, and I was here for an interview. We'd all been very competitive in our troop. Special forces make for a deep bond because of the need to trust each other implicitly. "A certain outfit that Royal bought for Christmas that first year we were all based in Iran. Whoever loses has to wear it for a full day. Christmas will be here soon enough."

Raucous laughter filled the room as Austin slapped the arm of the chair. "Let's hope they still have it on that site because you're gonna look hot in that!"

"Don't count on it."

"You haven't heard the challenge yet!"

At that moment, the door opened to reveal a man who looked like a cat who'd gotten all the damn cream as he stopped, a smile stretching over his face. "Well, I'll be damned. Wes! How the fuck are you? And what are you doing here and why didn't you tell me he was coming?" He directed the latter to Austin.

I got up to hug Warner. He smelled of something sweet and a masculine aftershave. "I'm here for an interview, only it seems Austin hasn't gotten over his competitive side."

Arms, solid with muscle, held me in a bear hug I remembered could make a guy feel a little less alone. "An interview. You thinking about joining us in the world of kink security?" His warm chuckle brushed my cheek as he pulled back and gave me the same appraisal Austin had. "You'll fit right in. You still got a hankering for a boy of your own, or have you met someone?"

A pretty blond with the cutest smile wearing fox ears popped into my mind as I shook my head. "Nope, I'm still single." A heavy feeling at admitting that came from how much, since I'd seen the blond, I'd struggled to think about trying to date anyone else.

Since our first meeting, I'd encountered him once more in the same spot. That first time, I'd stopped dead in my tracks to stare. He'd looked so damn beautiful I'd been captivated from the first instance. When he'd spoken for a moment, I'd thought he was talking to me until I realized his eyes were shut behind the lenses of his sunglasses. Unable to jog away without checking he was okay, I'd spoken.

So much about the way he presented himself told me a lot about him. The second time, I'd found him in the same spot wearing a similar outfit to the first. Only the fox ears were missing. We'd chatted a little longer, and I was planning to jog through the park again on Saturday to see if he came back. Last week there'd been no sign of him and I'd been more disappointed than I should have been.

"We lost you there?"

A hand waved in front of my face and I grinned, shamefaced to admit that they had when it was clear by Warner's head tilt he'd asked me something. "Sorry, what did you say?"

"That maybe I could introduce you to—"

"No setups, please. I remember the last time. Harvey was... interesting." I shuddered for effect, recalling the guy who liked to top from the bottom and had a voice that was worse than nails being dragged down a blackboard.

"Oh fuck, I forgot about that," Warner said around a grin that suggested he'd forgotten nothing and wasn't in the least bit sorry for one of the worst dates I'd ever been on.

"I'll stick to finding a boy for myself. Thanks for the offer, though."

Warner went to the other large desk in the room and sat behind it, then leaned to the side and looked out the window, waving.

I frowned at Austin.

"Oh, don't mind him. Remember Liam's son, Terrence" I nodded. "He's Warner's boyfriend. Terrence works from Liam's home so Warner can get to see his boy anytime he's free," Austin griped.

I gawked at Warner. "Does Liam know what you are into?"

"Yep. It's taken some adjustment on Terrence's part as he hid that side of himself until Liam's lawyer got wind and set the cat amongst the pigeons."

"Doesn't sound good," I replied to Warner's scowl.

"It wasn't, but thanks to Austin's skills on a computer and digging for information, we contained the situation." Something suggested that they'd done a little more than contain the problem, but I didn't pry. They'd tell me if they wanted me to know. And I was still processing that Liam lived next door and that his son was dating Warner.

"Was this when Liam was missing?" I'd heard about Liam's disappearance from secondhand sources as I was deep undercover.

"Yeah. It was a right shit show. Liam was in terrible shape when they found him and is still working on his recovery. I'm sure he'd love a visit."

"I'll call there when I'm finished here." I winked at Austin before looking at Warner. "And then I can check out Terrence. If I remember, he was a real sweetheart."

The scowl was back and aimed at me. "You won't go checking out anything."

"Shall we get back to why you're here?" Austin interjected with a light of amusement in his eyes.

"Let's," Warner said, shuffling papers on his desk. "Now, when can you start?"

Austin shook his head and rolled his eyes at Warner, then grinned at me. "What he said."

Chapter Two

Matty

Was it wrong to stick out my tongue at another employee? Why, yes, it was. Did I care? Absolutely not. I watched my ex and the guy he'd cheated on me with go down the corridor arm in arm after rubbing my nose in the fact they'd just gotten engaged. They deserved much worse but I was too much of a gentleman.

"A-hole," I muttered crossly, giving in to the need to express a little of how I was feeling, even if it wasn't to Peter or Richard. Stomping back down the thickly carpeted hallway into my office, I was glad that nearly everyone had left for the day.

It had been a hit and run by the pair. They'd surprised me because usually putrid Peter wanted an audience to dig the knife into an old wound. One that Peter, for whatever reason, tried to open at any opportunity of late.

I closed my office door, reminding myself I didn't like him anymore and he couldn't hurt me. When the hurt lingered, I sagged against the wood and stared unseeingly at my space. Only instead of the well-appointed office I'd lovingly decorated, all I could see was the image of Richard bouncing up and down on Peter's cock the night I'd caught them out.

Straightening away from the door, I resisted stooping to Peter's level and focused on it being Saturday the following day, and that I had a date in Milton Lee Olive park. Okay, not a date, as I wasn't sure my jogger friend would appear. And on the couple of occasions we'd met, there was nothing 'datish' about the time we spent together.

Rolling my eyes to the ceiling at how ridiculous I was being, it didn't stop the little quiver of excitement that came from the thought of seeing the hot, sexy jogger again. I'd not had that feeling for the last couple of guys I'd gone on dates with.

I hoped that after seeing him that second time, wearing yet another set of skimpy jogging wear, that the park was maybe a regular place he went to exercise. Not that I could hold that against him, some folks loved to do that sort of thing. I shuddered at the very idea.

Had he looked for me last week?

I'd missed the week before as I'd gone out with Gaines on a play date to Terrence's house, so there was no chance to test my theory. And as fun as the day with my friends had turned out, when I'd got home I'd become a little maudlin. Seeing what I didn't have was hard, especially when Austin and Warner had played with us. Oh, they'd included me, they weren't the type to exclude me from the play time.

Only I'd felt the prick of envy for my friends' relationships with their Daddies. Happy as I was for both Gaines and Terrence, it was hard nonetheless when I came home alone.

I'd turned down the offer to go again this week and told a half lie about plans at the park. I didn't think it was a full lie; I was going to the park on a date... just with myself.

The guilty feelings at not being honest with Gaines didn't sit right with me, and putrid Peter being all bubbly and happy didn't help my plight either. Seeing it was going to spoil my weekend if I let it, I went to my desk and closed all the files I'd opened on my computer and switched it off.

Gathering all my belongings, I did what I didn't do at home—unless Austin told me too—I tidied up my desk. Satisfied, I headed back out of the office, bag slung over my shoulder. The quiet revealed I was the last to leave once more. The firm I worked for was in a suburb of Chicago, Lake Zurich. Product Development Technologies was where I'd started my career as a design researcher. It was challenging and demanding in ways that left me often needing to go home to decompress. It was why I'd thought dating Peter when I'd met him out in a kink club was a good thing, as he'd get the work pressures I was under.

He hadn't!

Could I live with putrid Peter's beaming smile for the next... however long? Inside the bag slung over my shoulder were my fox ears and as much as I wanted to slip them on to make me feel better, I resisted as I left the building and went to get the commuter rail home. Once before, some thugs had made fun of me and snatched my ears off my head to break them. It was always an adventure on a Friday, so I wasn't taking any chances with my favorite set today.

Having hit the time of the ride home to perfection, I got a seat and hadn't had to endure someone who was ripe after a day in a stuffy office.

The five-minute walk to my home coincided with the sun dipping in the sky. It turned everything above me into beautiful shades of pink. The breathtaking sight lifted my mood when it came with thoughts of potentially eating whatever meal Austin had prepared alfresco.

He was all about healthy food choices and insisted I also eat the good stuff and reduce all the sugary treats I liked. Often, I'd take those treats in my work bag and eat them out of Austin's sight so as not to get a lecture. I liked him a lot, but there was a limit when it came to curbing my sweet tooth.

I'd barely stepped a foot inside the door when Gaines came up the stairs that led down to his pole dancing studio. He was dripping with sweat and flushed, wearing skimpy shorts and a white vest declaring in hot magenta 'a pole is the perfect place to mount'. He grinned widely, all teeth and happiness as he came at me at speed.

"Perfect timing. Daddy has made us cheese burgers with those sweet potato fries and dip you like," he gushed, stopping briefly to kiss my cheek, leaving it wet. A whiff of sweat lingering behind him before he ran for the stairs up to the bedrooms.

"Eww, you know I don't like to get sweaty!" I exclaimed, struggling to keep the laughter in when he wiggle danced up the stairs.

In a dramatic pose, he stopped at the top of the stairs, hand to forehead as he leaned back like he was swooning. "Why, I declare, my sweaty ass is sorry for touching you so inappropriately."

Gales of laughter erupted out of me as he bowed, then disappeared out of sight, laughing as hard as me. "You're not funny," I called out through my laughter.

"Then why are you laughing?" he shouted back.

Austin appeared from the kitchen, his expression showing his amusement. "He get you with his sweat again?"

I rubbed at my cheek, dropping my bag in the hallway, coming towards him. "He knows it bugs me."

He flipped a finger over my nose, chuckling. "We all know how much you like to avoid getting sweaty."

"I don't mind getting sweaty"—my eyes twinkled at him—"if it's in the right circumstances."

He held up a hand as if defending himself as I giggled. "No, please, I don't need to know about that."

Enjoying his playfulness, I batted my eyelashes at him, knowing he wouldn't take it to mean anything other than what it was. Harmless fun. "You sure?" I slipped my arm through his. "Did you know the Kama Sutra has some very energetic poses that can more than get a person... *moist*?"

He roared with laughter and shuddered at the same time. There was something about the word 'moist' he didn't like, and I couldn't help but tease him when the opportunity arose.

"Gross."

Continuing to giggle, I guided him back into the kitchen. "It's just a word," I said, all innocence.

"It's what it conjures." He unthreaded his arm and went to the table, pulling out a seat for me.

He was caring, and it was these little touches that made it difficult to not crave this with someone.

A finger rubbed at the top of the bridge of my nose. "Why the frown? Is everything okay?"

The seriousness of his tone made it hard to resist talking about my day. "Putrid Peter got engaged and came to rub my face in it with Richard."

He crouched at the side of the chair, his expression revealing his concern as his brow furrowed. "The ex you work with, right?"

"Yeah." I sighed and gave in to the temptation to spill my guts. "I figured something was going on with how the two of them have been in the office of late. Initially, they weren't so obvious with the touchy feely stuff. Then it was like they couldn't keep their hands off each other. Like a pair of dogs in heat."

Austin's lips twitched. "Dogs in heat, erm."

"They were dry humping in the supply closet, or so I heard. Thankfully, I didn't have to witness that. Not that I haven't seen them both naked doing it." I rubbed a finger over a droplet of condensation created by the ice inside a glass on the table, which must have been Austin's. "And that is a sight I'd like to bleach from my head."

"Is there any way to avoid them for a little while, until the excitement dies down?"

"What excitement dies down?" Gaines asked as he came into the kitchen, looking much less sweaty in clean shorts and baggy koala T-shirt.

"Putrid Peter got engaged."

Across the room in seconds, Gaines wrapped his arms around my shoulders and laid his chin on top of my head. "I'm sorry."

"I'm over him. It's just hard to watch them be all happy when..."

Gaines let go and came to sit on the seat next to me, looking directly at me. "You don't have a Daddy?"

It was easier to nod when my chin trembled, and I blinked back the tears that wanted to spill down my cheeks. I hated being like this. I wasn't this guy.

Moving once more, Gaines all but sat on my lap as Austin wrapped his muscular arms around us both. "What can we do to help?" Austin asked.

I couldn't see his face as Gaines was obscuring my view, but I knew the tone and he was serious.

"What Daddy said. What can we do to help?"

"This. This is good." Aiming to lighten the somber mood I'd created, I twisted as much as I could to look past Gaines at Austin. "Ice cream for dinner. That's good too."

He chuckled, and Gaines shook with silent laughter, crushing me to the chair. "Hey, you're squashing me!"

"You can have ice cream,"—I grinned at him as he let go and Gaines got up off me—"when you've eaten your burger, okay. I'll even give you an extra scoop for being a good boy and not complaining."

I sagged and gave him an exaggerated pout. "Alright, but if I eat all my burger, then I want three scoops of fish food."

Austin eyed me and shook his head. "I've no clue where you store it all."

I patted my flat tummy, grinning widely. "Right here."

"He's got hollow legs," Gaines supplied, reaching for the glass on the table to take a big drink from it, only to grimace when he swallowed. "Ewww, iced coffee." The glass went back on the table as he glared at it.

I snort-laughed when he then rushed to the refrigerator—his tongue poking out of his mouth like he couldn't bear it to be inside—opening it hard enough to make everything rattle inside the door. He pulled out a bottle of juice, took the lid off and gulped straight from the bottle.

Austin, who was now at the counter chopping up salad that I was well aware he was going to hide in my burger bun, stared at Gaines in such a way no words were needed.

The bottle got lowered and Gaines gave him a sheepish smile. "Sorry, Daddy. I'll get a glass." His nose wrinkled. "But I needed to get the awful taste out of my mouth."

"I'm sure Austin could have helped with that," I supplied cheekily, loving how both men glowed with rosy blushes.

"You said you wanted ice cream after dinner... right?"

There was enough of his Daddy voice to make me giggle. "I'll behave... *maybe*."

Chapter Three

Weston

Double checking the contents of the backpack I'd found online the week before, I nodded approval at how it worked for what I had planned for my day. The backpack was specific for runners and I hoped it would make it less obvious that I'd bought it so I could carry a snack box. I'd made one up after paying attention the previous week to what was lying next to my... *to Matty.*

I was having to remind myself daily he wasn't 'my boy' when my thoughts drifted towards the blond elf who frequented more and more of them. No amount of wanting him as my boy was going to get me pushing him. Something about Matty called to me. I wanted to get to know him, to get him to see he could trust me while I figured out what had put that sad smile on his face. He hid whatever was bothering him behind a cheekiness that was extremely appealing. There was just something else lurking beneath the smile that I wanted to explore and ease.

There was a sense of wariness to him sometimes that I was positive came from being hurt. Keeping things light on these non-date dates—because these Saturday meetings were no longer by chance—was getting harder. Four weeks in a row we'd met in the secret garden with no one else around, making the place feel like ours. Each time, I'd lingered a little longer, going in full length running pants these past two weeks so I could stay out in the cooling fall weather.

We'd so far chatted about the hidden gardens in Chicago and what inspired him to find them, as well as his love of foxes and the zoo he'd visited with friends. I'd wanted to ask if one friend was a boyfriend but I'd held back. I got the impression he was single, otherwise why would he be frequenting parks alone?

The need for him to *want* to share because it was his choice and not because I pushed him increased with each encounter. The more I learned about him, the more smitten I grew. It had taken him two weeks before he'd shared his name. Although when I called him pumpkin, he didn't seem to mind, judging by how he brimmed with happiness. That was more contagious than any virus and I yearned to see him happy.

The fox ears had been missing last week, so I'd done some shopping and I tucked my purchase next to the juice cartons and packet of fruit sticks, making sure they didn't get squashed. Happy I had everything, I slipped the backpack over my shoulders, tightened the straps so it wouldn't move when I jogged and checked I'd not forgotten anything as I slipped a key into the zipped part at the back of my running pants.

Out the door of my apartment moments later, adrenaline buzzed through me like I was heading off on a mission. I was. But this mission could hurt a part of me I'd kept safe throughout my life—my heart. It was a sobering thought as I entered the elevator.

When it stopped on the sixth floor, I smiled politely at the couple who got on. I didn't know many of the people who lived in the large apartment block. I'd not been home long enough in the past to get acquainted with anyone.

The only noise was that of the soft elevator music playing as we descended. That awkwardness of being inside a box with folks I didn't know didn't compel me to fill the silence. At the reception level, I waited for them to exit ahead of me before I followed.

I nodded at Burt. He'd staffed the large reception desk for as long as I'd lived in the building, and I'd learned to hurry through the lobby if I didn't want to get caught up in a conversation about politics. As I didn't want to be late for my non-date, I offered a polite smile and kept going.

Last week, Matty appeared to be waiting for me. In the same spot I'd found him before, his face remained turned in the direction I jogged from. A smile had spread slowly, lighting his eyes when he'd seen me appear. It had stolen my breath faster than any exercise could. I was eager to see if it was the same this week.

A frown appeared as I recalled the difference in him, which I hadn't noticed at first. When I realized he'd chopped at his curls, my stomach had dipped with disappointment to see most of them gone. His bangs had some curls left. He'd spent a lot of time running a hand through his hair as if self-conscious, so I'd kept my questions about why he'd decided on the change to myself and directed the conversation to what he liked to do besides visit parks and the zoo.

The breeze was a little stiffer coming off Lake Michigan as I started jogging toward the park. It wasn't far and my muscles quickly warmed as I quickened my pace, anticipation joining the high of exercising that I always got.

I'd barely winded myself when Matty came into view. The trees were losing their leaves and allowed the sun to poke through the canopy above his head. Sun snuck past the thick, fluffy clouds to bounce off his blond hair, highlighting golden threads that glistened in the brightness. He reminded me of a late summer flower in bloom.

I slowed my pace to admire the picture he made. Today, he wore a thick jumper in heather green with chocolate brown jeans tucked into a small ankle boot of the same color. Again, the fox ears were missing and it left me with an unsettled feeling.

Quickening my pace once more, my sneakers slapped on the path and drew his gaze from the water. The beaming happiness at the sight of me was immediate. Back was the giddy feeling bubbling up right in the center of my chest, making me respond in kind to his grin.

"Hey," I called out. "You beat me again."

As I came to a stop, his head tilted. "Mom is a stickler for timekeeping. It kinda stuck."

My pulse leapt at his acknowledgement that we had a time to meet, whether or not it was official. "People who are always late is one of my pet peeves. It shows a lack of consideration for the other person, don't you think? And that isn't nice and could garner a punishment." I couldn't resist giving him more hints about me. I softened the words, while making sure he knew I was serious.

His brows rose a fraction and a light of interest appeared in his eyes. "Punishment?" He shivered, and I wasn't quite sure if he was cold or considering what that meant to me.

"No one wants to get their bottom spanked for being late, do they?"

His cheeks became flooded with delicate pink as his eyelashes dipped and for a brief second he sucked his lower lip between his teeth, chewing on it. "Don't suppose so."

He didn't sound convinced, and I stored that tidbit of information away for later while I came to sit next to him on the grass. It was cool beneath my ass, penetrating the thin fabric of my pants. It was a sharp contrast to the heat coming from him, along with a floral scent he seemed to favor. It was one I'd not yet been able to find in any store.

As I removed my backpack, he eyed it with curiosity. "What have you got in there?"

I opened the zipper, and he came closer, his body brushing against the side of mine as he tried to peer into the backpack. I moved it to the side, out of his direct eyeline, and tutted. "It's a surprise."

He wiggled against me. "A surprise for me?" he asked excitedly as his attention shifted from what I held, to me. It was hard to resist his eagerness as he looked shyly up at me from under his eyelashes. "What is it?"

"Does that look always work, to get what you want?" I asked around my laughter at the pout that had formed when I kept the backpack right where it was.

"Sometimes." He pressed a tiny bit closer, and my heart crashed into my ribcage. "Is it working Da... Weston?"

The slip up warmed me to the soles of my feet. There was nothing that would convince me he wasn't about to call me Daddy. My chuckle was throaty as I shook my head. "I'm made of stronger stuff than that."

With a look that seemed to be all consideration, he eyed me up and down with a hunger that he didn't mask. "I'm sure you are."

His husky voice and his expression were like a caress to my dick, and it took concerted effort not to react to either. The pants I wore would conceal nothing. Needing a distraction that wasn't the once more pouty lips, I dug into the backpack.

He came closer still, until he was all but sitting in my lap, trying to see what I'd hidden inside. I reached for the pretty fox ears and turned to hold his stare as I brought them out to offer them to him.

With him pressed against me, I could feel the immediate tension in his body when he stiffened.

Fuck. Fuck. Have I fucked up?

His chin quivered and his eyes widened to the point they seemed to consume his whole face. "You got those for me?" he whispered.

I wasn't sure what to make of his breathless, trembling tone.

"I noticed you were missing them last week and you... look so happy when you wear them..." I trailed off when two fat tears rolled down his cheeks and he hiccuped out a sob before his fisted hand went to his lips.

I dropped the fox ears onto my lap and used my thumbs to brush away the tears, holding his chilly cheeks in my palms. "Oh pumpkin, I didn't mean to upset you."

He gave a very undignified sniff and wiped the back of his hand over his nose, dislodging my hands as he shook his head and I let go.

"I'm not upset," he hiccuped, his breath hitching.

Despite what he said, the knots that formed in my shoulders—that weighed heavier than a training pack in the army—didn't ease. How could I become convinced when two more tears rolled down his cheeks, reaching his chin before I could stop them?

"Then why the tears?" I asked softly, needing to understand.

Chapter Four

Matty

It had been so long since I'd had anyone—besides Gaines and he didn't count because he was my best friend—notice something important to me and want to do something nice for me.

My heart was beating so rapidly I wasn't sure it wouldn't just burst like an alien right out of my chest, like in the movie. How could I explain why I wasn't wearing my fox ears?

Before I realized what I was about to do, my lips parted and it all tumbled out. "Putrid Peter caught me in the restroom at work wearing my favorite fox ears because he and his fiancé have taken immense pleasure in rubbing my nose in their wedding plans. Every time I turn around, they're there talking about how eager they are to get married. If that wasn't bad enough, they've actually been dating while I was stupidly blind to what was going on behind my back when Peter and I were dating. I've never even considered how long they were getting down and dirty, laughing behind my back. I just wanted to forget it. Get over it with how hurt I'd been by the betrayal."

A deep furrow appeared between Weston's brows before his head tilted and his lips pinched together in such a way that suggested he was mad about something. He remained silent, as if encouraging me to continue to get it all out. Or that's what my heart wanted to believe, so everything I'd held tightly on to, for far too long, spilled from my lips. I'd put on a brave smile at home, avoiding spending any real time with Gaines and Austin, knowing it would only upset Gaines. He was so happy right now; I didn't want to spoil it with my angsty feelings.

They had sat inside me, churning my guts, and making these meetings with Weston my only bright spot in the week. These chance meetings—sort of dates—were what got me through the last two weeks. I didn't want to appear clingy or needy and scare him off. That didn't appear to stop me today, though.

"Now everyone in the office knows how foolish I've been." A sob rose and I choked it back, recalling how embarrassed I'd been the week before. "I overheard someone laughing about the dating inconsistency and I needed to feel better." I sniffed again. "So I went and hid in the restroom. The one that was furthest away that folks don't like to walk to, but putrid Peter found me."

I slumped, hating how I couldn't escape the fact I'd made such a horrible error of judgment. "Then he started ridiculing me about wearing my fox ears. He snatched them off my head and flung them on the floor... and they broke." I sniffed even louder, struggling to hold back the next bout of tears, wanting to spill.

Blinking hard at the memory of watching them bouncing off the sink and hitting the wall where the band had snapped in half made that impossible and they fell down my cheeks.

"That little shithead!" he exclaimed, his eyes snapping with anger.

Before I could figure what he was going to do, he picked up the band with the gorgeous fox ears attached that looked almost identical to the ones Peter broke. He came so close I could scent his masculine fragrance as he carefully placed them on my head. His fingers brushed at the few remaining curls I'd left after going to the salon to make myself feel better. The fresh look I'd let myself get talked into made me feel vulnerable for reasons I couldn't actually verbalize. It wasn't me and without my favorite ears—I felt lost.

As the band settled on my head, I felt a strange, euphoric feeling in the pit of my stomach. I stared in wonder at the man who understood this side of me and wasn't in the slightest put off by it. Through blurry eyes, I watched him pull out his cell phone and flick the screen to use the camera. My eyes widened at him brushing a few strands around the ears. His smile warmed and his anger disappeared as he admired his handy work. "There. That's better, pumpkin."

He encouraged me to look at myself on the camera's screen and a fluttery feeling joined the euphoric one. Although I had a red nose and teary eyes, I looked more like me with the pretty ears and the way he'd strategically placed my remaining curls.

The feelings in my tummy increased as he gently stroked away the remaining stray tear on my cheek with the pad of his thumb. I watched him suck the thumb into his mouth, my reflection no longer what I became focused on but the tendrils of desire at the sight of Weston sucking his thumb between plump lips, tasting my tears.

A whimper passed over my lips without permission at thoughts of using his thumb instead of my binky. His gaze focused completely on me. The moment lengthened until my chest burned from holding my breath at the intensity of his focus.

For a second, I thought he was going to kiss me; I wanted him to. I wanted it more than I'd ever wanted anything in my life. A work roughened palm cupped the side of my face. "Your ex doesn't deserve your tears."

"No, he doesn't," I mumbled, doing my best not to move to dislodge the hand that connected us. "It's been nearly a year since we split up and I am over him." My shoulders sagged when it didn't sound like it after everything I'd just said.

Would Weston think I remained hung up on another guy?

"It's just having to see putrid Peter seeming to get pleasure out of my distress…" The moment I said it aloud, it struck me as was what was giving me the biggest upset. "For some reason, I feel as if Peter is targeting me, and I don't understand why. I didn't cheat on him. I dumped him, yes, because I would never let myself get used like that." I met a concerned stare. "So, why is he picking on me?"

It wasn't like Weston could answer me, only I wanted him to, because I saw him as my… *Daddy*.

"I'm not sure I can answer that without it coming off as biased. I suspect he wants to have his cake and eat it, too. You're beautiful and I would find it hard to part with such a special… boy." The rough pad of his finger ran down the edge of my jawline as his hand slid away, increasing my shivers of desire.

He thinks I'm beautiful!

A special boy.

My shivers increased but had nothing to do with the fall weather or drop in temperature. When he eased away and twisted to reach for his pack, I exhaled shakily. The desperate need to feel his lips on mine made me squirm and him glance back. His brow quirked up?

Feeling way too exposed, I offered him the cell phone I was still holding.

He took it, his eyes narrowing on me as I forced a smile on my lips. After a pause, he tucked the phone into the pack he held in his other hand. He settled it on his lap and I wished more than anything that I was that pack.

I was distracted a moment later when he brought out a snack box with a small fox face on it and a silly grin appeared on my face.

The fizzy drink feeling bubbling inside me was back. "Did you bring me a snack box?"

~/~/~/~

Cold and shivering, I entered my home, heading through to the kitchen, trying not to focus on the fact that I'd lingered far too long in the garden just to be close to Weston. I needed a hot chocolate to warm me up.

I pulled up short in the doorway at the sight of Gaines wrapped in Austin's arms. His head was resting on his shoulder and Austin was rocking him gently. Everything about the scene spoke of their connection. Of their love. I wanted that so badly that an ache developed in the center of me as I imagined Weston doing the same thing to me.

The snack box and the fox ears, the care he took to listen to me, suggested he was indeed a Daddy, but I'd once more chickened out of asking after the afternoon's emotional rollercoaster.

I stepped back, hoping to escape before either man spotted me, only to hit one of the creaky floorboards just outside the kitchen. Gaines' head popped up, and he twisted to look at me.

There was upset clearly defined in the lines around his lips and red, puffy eyes. Retracing my steps, I entered the kitchen.

"What is it? What happened? Why are you crying?" I asked in a rush, dropping my small bag onto the counter. My concern for Gaines was my only focus.

"Your ears... they're new," he squeaked out while wriggling in Austin's arms to get put down. On the floor, he rushed to me and gave me a big hug.

I looked over his shoulder at Austin. "Speak to him," he mouthed, then walked past us and out of the kitchen.

Oh no, he was upset with me.

"I'm sorry. What did I do to upset you?" I whispered, hugging him hard. He smelled of lemons and something sweet.

"Why aren't you talking to me 'bout what's wrong? We always tell each other everything," he said, pulling away from me. His big, watery eyes held a light of accusation I couldn't avoid.

I blew out a noisy breath and guided him to the table, taking a seat on the bench and tugging him down next to me. "Putrid Peter has been rubbing my nose in his wedding plans and he broke my fox ears."

After talking this through with Weston, the earlier upset wasn't quite so 'stabby' this time, as I explained everything that had happened over the last few weeks.

He got a light in his eyes that I didn't often see—anger. "Why, that asshole! How dare he torture you like that. We're gonna fix him." He patted my hand and turned to face the doorway, shouting, "Dad-dyyyyyy."

"What? Why are you calling Austin?" I asked, getting more alarmed by the second at how determined my friend looked when Austin appeared a few seconds later.

"You bellowed, my sweet boy." Austin's grin suggested the Daddy voice he'd used was just for effect.

"Putrid Peter has been harassing Matty at work. You can help, can't you?" It wasn't a question. I knew my friend. He gave Austin the best begging face I'd ever seen.

I held up my hand. "It's fine, I'll deal with it. I talked it through with Weston—"

"He broke your favorite fox ears on purpose... that's... that's nasty. You don't have to put up with that. Does he Daddy?" The latter, he said in a wobbly voice, swinging from anger to upset with a crestfallen expression, which did nothing to help my plight. Then his gaze returned to me and I could see the second he registered the name I'd mentioned. "Who's Weston?"

I loved Gaines with all my heart and hated that I'd made him sad, but the accusatory tone said I was in deep trouble. I squirmed under a stare that suggested I needed to spill before there was bloodshed. "I met him at the park."

"Which park? And is that who you've been seeing on Saturdays when you won't come with me to play with Terrence? Why haven't you mentioned you're dating someone?"

Head shaking, I rushed to explain, "We're not dating. We meet in the park when he jogs through, that's all." We did, until today, when he bought me snacks and fox ears.

Would that class as a date?

If anyone witnessed the look Gaines wore right then, they'd never consider he could be the sweet boy he was with Austin. Austin's chuckle warned me things were about to get interesting as he took a seat at the far end of the kitchen table, which sat under the large window, as if preparing to watch a show.

"How many times have you met," his hands came up as he air quoted, "'while he's jogged'?"

"Seven times," I mumbled defensively.

"You're dating!" he said in a strangled voice.

I got up and stomped to the counter, then spun around, feeling far too defensive. "We aren't." I shook my head when he followed me, his lips parting. "I want to date him, don't get me wrong. We haven't gotten to the stage of him asking me out. Not that I'm saying he wants to, 'cause I'm not. We kind of meet, like randomly, every week in the park."

It sounded kooky to me and I could see why Gaines wasn't buying it, but I'd never lie to him. "It's the truth. Only today he bought me a snack box and..." my hand reached up to stroke the fox ears I'd not taken off, "these."

Gaines jabbed a finger at me. "Dating." He looked at Austin for confirmation. "Aren't they, Daddy?"

"He bought a gift and is catering to Matty's little side during these 'not official dates'. That says he's taking it slow, letting you get used to him. Sensible and caring. Yep, you're dating." Austin's expression turned serious as he came forward, pinching the end of his chin. "What did you say his name was?"

I wasn't sure, but there was something about the way Austin asked that suggested he already had the answer. "Weston. I didn't ask his last name." I glanced at Gaines when he made a choking noise, distracting me from Austin's widening grin. "'Cause we ain't dating. If we were, surely he'd have told me?" Like that made total sense to me, I nodded my head at Gaines.

"Do you want to date him?" This came from Austin.

"I just said I did," I answered without hesitation.

"Daddy, you know Matty attracts losers. If he hasn't given his last name to Matty, he might have six boyfriends all over Chicago," Gaines exclaimed dramatically.

"Thanks for the support," I snapped, and Gaines came over and slung an arm around my waist, hugging me close.

I eyed Austin with suspicion when he chuckled. "Why are you laughing?" He wasn't the kind to be hurtful, and laughing right now seemed inappropriate.

"I believe I can help with both scores."

Having lost track of the conversation, I stared at him and blinked in confusion. "Both scores?"

"Your ex. We'll come up with something to deal with the Peter issue and get him off your back at work."

I blinked slowly, staring at Austin, and the look of menace, mirrored by the tone of his voice, replaced the humor of moments ago. One that reminded me he'd been in the army and wasn't someone anyone would want to mess with. On one of the play dates with Terrence, he talked a little about his father, Liam, and how he'd commanded the unit both Austin and Warner, Terrence's Daddy, were in. I'd never met Liam, but he sounded scary to me and something about Austin suggested he could be just as scary, if pushed.

"Is that all right?" Austin questioned, looking at me.

I nodded and hoped that whatever I was agreeing to didn't require me doing anything too hard or that could get me fired.

"Great, I'll get it sorted for you." He got up and came to pat my shoulder, kissing Gaines' forehead. "Daddy will figure everything out, don't worry."

Did that include Weston, too?

Watching him retreat from the room, I got a feeling it did but I couldn't see how. I didn't want to appear desperate by asking when he'd offered to help with Peter.

The hand clutching my side squeezed, and I met Gaines' stare. "I've half an hour before my next class. Now fill me in and don't you dare leave out any of the details of your 'dates'."

Chapter Five

Weston

Knocking on the office door, I waited for Austin to call out before pushing it open and stepping inside.

The scent of wood, rich leather, and expensive aftershave were present but subtle as I walked to the chair in front of Austin's large desk. An iMac computer sat in front of Austin, whose fingers tapped quickly over the keys.

I glanced at Warner's empty desk and grinned when I checked the time. Warner spent his lunchtime in the building next door, with his boy. Austin had explained that Warner went to make sure his boy ate, otherwise Terrence would forget and allow work to take up all of his time. I suspected it was more that Warner liked to take care of his boy. I'd met Terrence twice. He was shy and clearly in love with Warner, loving the attention his Daddy gave him.

Leaning back a fraction, I looked out the window at the building next door while Austin continued to batter the keys. There, in the house's window next door, I could see Warner with his boy sat snuggled in his lap, just as I suspected. My pulse skipped several beats at how I could imagine me holding Matty exactly as Warner was doing with Terrence. The temptation at the weekend to do exactly that left me with a nasty bite on the inside of my cheek.

Everything about Matty called to me and fighting the attraction was getting harder. The weekend meeting had proven how deep and swift my feelings had grown for the boy. He'd shown me a level of trust by confessing what had upset him, one I didn't want to break by putting my own needs first, so I'd held them firmly in check. That didn't stop Matty from keeping me off kilter, though. I wasn't prepared to take a misstep by rushing him into something when he appeared to have unresolved issues with his ex, despite what he said.

Occupying my time, I replayed the conversation with him over and over, trying to figure out how to help without overstepping a mark I'd drawn. As yet, I'd come up with nothing that would not get me arrested when it involved shoving putrid Peter's teeth down his throat for hurting such a sweet boy as Matty.

"You can take a seat, you know."

The amusement in Austin's voice snapped me from my thoughts and I grinned at him, taking a seat in the chair I was standing behind. "I was just watching Warner and Terrence. I don't think I ever remember seeing him so content before," I said, which was initially where my thoughts had been.

Austin sat back in his leather seat, making it creak as he rocked in it, his fingers templing under his chin. "You're right." He nodded towards the large window. "He was smitten with the boy for three years before he made his move, and only then after a little nudge." His gaze narrowed when it returned to me.

I grinned at Austin, recalling what Warner had shared. That nudge was more of a shove, the same one Warner then gave Austin in Gaines direction. "You both like to meddle, and from what I hear, you needed a little help of your own."

Rich, hearty laughter filled the room. "I did. Only it wasn't just Warner who helped me with Gaines, but his best friend." His eyes narrowed on me and the hairs on the back of my neck rose.

"Whatever you're thinking, you can stop right now. I'm not interested in getting hooked up with anyone." Not unless it is an adorable blond boy who loves anything fox related and looked cute wearing fox ears.

He gave a hearty sigh, not looking in the least bit put off. "Are you sure? He's gorgeous—"

I waved him off before he could continue. "No, you can stop right there. I do not want you to hook me up, okay!"

His grin was wide and mischievous, despite his next words. "I hear you, no setups."

"Shall we get to the reason you asked me to come in? I have my planned work schedule. I picked it up from Warner on Friday."

"Yes, about that, I was hoping to add to it? I know you only wanted part-time hours, but something's come up." He lost the humor in his expression and a hard mask I'd seen a time or two slipped into place. "There's a situation happening to a young man where he's being harassed in his workplace. I'm not sure right now what the best plan of attack would be but I need someone to do some recon first. As this was—is your area of expertise, I thought you could help?"

My pulse skipping a beat at how it sounded like the situation Matty was dealing with, I nodded eagerly. I might not be able to help Matty… *yet,* but I could help this young man. "Tell me more."

An hour later, I left Austin's office with a sketchy outline of a situation and bare bones details on Peter Foulkes. Something niggled at the back of my thoughts about the similarities and the name of the guy. I quickly passed it off as a coincidence. It wasn't like there weren't hundreds, if not thousands, of men in Chicago called Peter.

The odd feeling in my gut didn't subside and after running through everything I'd gleaned, there was nothing to suggest I was missing anything. I shoved aside the unsettled feeling and once more put it down to the similarities to Matty's shitty situation while I headed to my car.

Having no plans for the afternoon and not one to waste time, I drove to the address I'd put in my Sat Nav. One Corporate Drive in a suburb geared more to families than big business was not what I'd expected.

Parking up on Kemper Drive, I exited the car. The briskness of the air coming from the lake pulled at my jacket while I walked under a dull gray sky, listening to the sounds of bird cries above me. Product Development Technologies design studio was easy to find. A modern building positioned to allow a view of the lake from either side was situated in the heart of a golfer's paradise. Head of global operations, the place was smaller than I expected, making it easy to stroll around the perimeter unobtrusively.

Burned orange and russet red tree leaves crunched under the soles of my shoes as I walked around, nodding to those who passed wheeling golf buggies. Finding a seat that gave me an unobstructed view of the parking lot, I inhaled the fresh air.

Prepared to stay for a while, I took out my cell phone and checked my emails. As promised, Austin, who was a whizz at digging into people's lives on the internet, had sent several links to Peter Foulkes' social media pages. Instagram had a mine of information.

Objectively, I could see the dude was mildly attractive. He had styled his dark, graying hair to make the most of a weak-looking jawline. Eyes of pale blue were meh and his build was average. There was an attention to detail in the way he dressed. The dude clearly didn't do causal and the smile he aimed at the camera—which he appeared to have an affair with considering the number of head shot selfies—revealed teeth that were too perfect to be his own.

The second man in the shots was pretty in a conventional sense, though there was nothing appealing about him to me. Since meeting Matty, there was no one who could offer the brightness that came from within him, which had so easily captivated me.

The couple in the photos lacked what I'd consider a genuine connection. The moments captured were all... contrived. Nothing about them spoke to a realism that suggested a deeper bond between a couple who—I glanced at the status bar—were engaged.

A skipping pulse got me scrolling further down the page, only to reach the end and find no other pictures of anyone I recognized. A rush of air left my chest as I moved on to Facebook, feeling relieved and not wanting to focus on why.

The sound of voices brought me from my deep dive into social media sometime later, and three things registered. The gray was now more pronounced than it had been, showing how long I'd been sitting,

I was cold, and it had reached clocking off time, judging by the number of folks exiting the building in front of me.

It didn't take long to spot Peter. Only it wasn't him who held my attention, but the man who held onto his arm. The air arrested in my chest. *Peter works with his fiancé?* Back to playing over the commonalities between Matty and Peter, I stared at the building, waiting.

What felt like an eternity later, with how my lungs refused to work, I leaned forward at the sight of a familiar blond haired sweetie strolling out of the building. Although dressed in slim fitting, cherry colored slacks with a fitted white button down, black boots and a jacket, there remained something non-conservative about Matty as he came to a halt in the throng of people. His blond head twisted towards the car lot, to where I'd watched Peter go with Richard. Before I could gauge what he was thinking, Matty hurriedly headed off in the opposite direction.

Up and following behind, the reason I was there slipped from my mind as chaos ruled.

Was this a set-up by Austin?

An earlier gut reaction to this situation proved I'd not lost my ability to pick up on something that was hokey.

Who was really behind this set-up? Austin? Matty?

I didn't believe for one minute it was Matty behind this. No. My interfering friends were more likely when I recalled the mischievous look Austin wore when he'd mentioned his boy's friend and I'd shut the conversation down. Was Matty the one Austin had planned to set me up with? As much as I wanted to kick Austin's ass, I really couldn't find anything wrong with his choice.

If it was Matty.

That begged another question. Did Matty know about me? About the work I did for Austin and Warner? Had Austin told Matty who would deal with his problem? Austin had been clear, their client—Matty—knew someone was going to deal with Peter.

Again, it felt like a 'no' with how Austin and Warner liked to meddle, it would seem, in other's business. But I continued to follow Matty, keeping my distance, leaving my car where I'd parked it.

If Matty suspected anyone was following him, he didn't let on. I'd found a seat in the back of the train that allowed me to observe Matty, who had his back to me, staring out the window and wearing a thoughtful expression. Even from where I was sitting, I could see his brow scrunched up in the glass window's reflection. I resisted the temptation to accidentally—on purpose—bump into him.

When he exited the train, I followed, keeping some commuters between us for as long as possible. Matty's pace quickened when we reached the street. It was harder to blend, so I had to fall back some.

I slipped my hand into my slacks and pulled out my cell phone, checking the address Austin had given me for him, then put it into google maps. One glance at the street name of where I was confirmed exactly where Matty was leading me to.

When the front door of the large home shut and concealed Matty, I considered my options.

Big bay windows overlooked a well-maintained garden closed in with wrought-iron railings. Wood painted in cream and fawn gave the place a well-cared for appearance. The porch was small, with several steps leading up to it. I ran through what Matty had shared about himself. Hadn't he mentioned he lived with his best friend? Was that best friend Gaines, Austin's boyfriend?

Scrolling through my contacts, I walked past the house and went to the corner, keeping out of view, and dialed Austin's number.

"Hey Wes, everything okay?" Austin asked, sounding distracted by whoever was talking in the background.

Could I hear Matty?

"You home?" I replied, instead of answering his question.

"Yeah, why?"

It was easy to hear the confusion in his voice while I came to a decision and headed back to the house, opening the gate, and walking up path to the steps. "Great, let me in then. I think you and I have something to discuss."

Chapter Six

Matty

"Whatsup with Austin?" I asked, watching him leave the kitchen in a hurry, with a frown on his face and his phone to his ear.

Gaines shrugged and took my bag off the counter where I'd placed it. "Must be something work related." He dropped it onto the floor, his brows drawing together when it clunked on the tiles, reminding me I'd slipped my metal sippy cup inside before leaving the office. "What have you got in here, rocks?"

A giggle bubbled out. "Don't be silly, it's just the new sippy cup I found. It's metal, but it had this super cute bat-eared fox on it."

He quickly had the bag back in his hand, rooting inside, making my smile widen. Neither of us had any boundaries with each other, though Gaines was much tidier than me. "Did you notice if they had one with a koala bear on?" he asked while inspecting the cup and lid with the small spout that made it easy to sip at.

"Didn't see one, though I'll admit when I saw the fox one I didn't take the time to see what else they had. I've got the web address if you want..." Mouth open as if catching flies, what we'd been discussing flew right out of my head as I swung to look at the doorway, where I could hear voices.

No way!

Multiple shivers ran through me and warmed my skin.

Weston!

How was Weston here?

I darted to the door and came to an abrupt halt to prevent smashing straight into Weston's chest. The coldness coming from him didn't make any difference to me with how hot I ran from the gorgeous smile tugging at his lips. It sent all kinds of warm fuzzies through me.

"What are you doing here?" I asked in a breathy, shocked voice. One that suggested I'd run some distance, not the ten paces across the kitchen.

Weston glanced back at Austin and one brow arched at him. A look passed between them that I couldn't read, setting off a riot of folks wearing spiked heels tramping around inside my stomach.

Austin stepped around Weston, going to Gaines, who'd laid my bag and cup down. Austin slipped an arm around Gaines' waist and pulled him close. The smile he wore didn't help my poor stomach. "Weston is the person helping deal with your issue with Peter."

"He works for you?" I squeaked out like a strangled cat, alarm making sure my face could heat the room. It felt like I'd become a glow stick that was illuminating the room all on its own.

Had Weston known all along who I was? The next thought caused ice to follow the heat. Had he played me? At the very idea, pain slashed through my chest. I stepped back from him, instinctively needing to protect myself from the hurt after everything I'd shared.

Following me into the kitchen, Weston threw a look at Austin that wasn't helping, although he respected the space I'd put between us.

His nod was stilted. "I do work for Austin and Warner. But before you assume otherwise, I didn't know of the connection between you and Austin until you exited the building I was watching this afternoon. What you told me on Saturday slotted in with why Austin asked me to do some recon on Peter."

"You followed me home." It wasn't a question, although his head inclined towards me. Conflicted by thoughts of him watching me while I'd been unaware, I eyed him, trying to recall what I'd done. A part of me was pleased that he had checked out where I lived. Whereas another part felt creeped out at not noticing him. Had I done anything to embarrass myself? There'd be nothing worse than if I'd picked my nose without thought or something equally awful. Although right then, I couldn't come up with anything worse.

"I wanted to confirm what I suspected." His gaze traveled to Austin, who shifted, looking uncomfortable.

Gaines, who'd been looking at Weston, tilted his head back to look up at Austin, his nose wrinkling, speaking to his annoyance. "Daddy, you knew who Matty was talking about the other day when you said you'd help. Why didn't you tell me? I thought we had a rule, no secrets unless they were for something special?" The snap to his voice was uncommon and, therefore, much more effective.

I didn't miss how Austin winced. "Don't you think this is special? I was helping Matty get what he wants." He sounded very persuasive, but the wrinkles never disappeared.

No matter, the high-heeled party goers in my stomach had upped their tempo inside me at what Austin inferred. Had he been attempting to get me Weston for a Daddy? Thrilled and terrified at thoughts of Weston thinking I'd set him up, I kept my gaze averted, watching him out of the corner of my eye instead. His gaze remained on Austin, who now looked as if he was sweating under the kitchen lights.

"You were interfering..." a grin appeared as if a thought had just occurred to Gaines, "like when Matty helped get me a date with you." The softness to his features and how dreamy eyed he'd gotten said it was time to distract them both, otherwise they'd be kissing next, which would lead to other stuff I didn't want to see. Once, I'd caught them making out in the kitchen and that was one too many times for me.

"I encouraged you to go and see him. I did not interfere," I said indignantly. When Gaines rolled his eyes at me, I shook my head. "I helped. I didn't interfere," I reiterated.

"Whatever you say." Gaines puckered up his lips at Austin.

"No, you don't start the kissy stuff. We have a guest, and I'm sure he's got questions for Austin." Ones I wanted to hear because it might help figure out if it pissed him off that Austin had set him up.

I finally got the courage to look directly at Weston, who was looking thoroughly amused if the smile he aimed at me was anything to go by. It gave me a little buzz, as if I'd stuck my finger in the wall socket and got a shock.

"I do." He sniffed at the air. "As something smells delicious, Austin can explain himself over dinner, then he can take me back to where I left my car." His tone suggested arguing with him wasn't an option, despite the gleam of humor that remained as he continued to smile at me.

With everyone helping and the conversation, by silent agreement, staying clear of the reason Weston was here and about to eat dinner with me, spaghetti and meatballs with herb bread got laid on the table twenty minutes later.

I usually sat on the bench with my back to the window. It was my favorite seat, but I hesitated, waiting to see where Weston sat, as I wanted to sit next to him. I didn't want to be obvious, yet it appeared I was when Gaines giggled looking at my seat, then back to where I remained standing. "Aren't you gonna sit?"

Weston, who'd placed the tray of drinks on the table, glanced at me. The pause was obvious enough to make me squirm.

"Pumpkin, do you want me to help you?"

The quiet question got more giggles from Gaines and an amused look from Austin, who looked at his friend like this was the first time he'd ever seen him.

"Eyes on me, Pumpkin." It was a soft command that was easy to obey. His brows arched. "Do you want... me to help you?"

Had he been about to call himself Daddy?

Not wanting to second guess myself or him, I nodded. Then, suddenly feeling shy, I dipped my gaze. Uncertainty on how to navigate this situation in my home *and* with an audience right there strummed at my nerves. Playing with Terrence and Gaines with their Daddies present was different. I wasn't Little right now, and I didn't want to confess that those I'd dated in the past hadn't been my Daddy once Little time was over.

I knew that all the men who worked for Austin and Warner were into kink because of what their business involved. So was I right about Weston being a Daddy? Was this him showing me?

He came around the table and eyed the bench then shifted the table carefully, so as not to spill anything. He created a gap big enough for me to slip in behind it with ease. Taking my normal seat, he came and sat next to me, moving the table back into place.

The brush of his flexing thigh against mine made it even more real. He reached for the bowl of spaghetti and lifted it, then silently forked some onto my plate while Gaines and Austin took the seats opposite us.

The silence around the table felt tense to me. Or it was me who was feeling tense with how Austin and Gaines watched Weston sort my meal wordlessly. Was it approval I could see in both men's gazes?

Once the sauce was on my spaghetti and he'd cut up some of the herb bread, he fixed his own plate. Thankfully, Austin turned his attention to Gaines, giving me some breathing room. Again, I waited to see what Weston would do next when everyone had food on their plates.

Austin often fed Gaines. It wasn't so much a conversational thing that decided whether this would occur, but more of a mood situation, I'd noticed.

Weston reached for my fork and swirled some spaghetti and sauce around it, offering it up to my lips with a gentle smile. Our gazes held and hope spiraled through me at what this was we were doing. I opened up, and he placed the fork in my mouth. I'm quite sure the food was tasty, but I couldn't have said so with any certainty. My entire focus was on the man taking the time to feed me and paying no attention to the men opposite us like it was something we did every day. One mouthful for me, then he'd eat a forkful.

This continued, but things got interesting when he deemed I needed a drink. With the snack box he'd made for me at the weekend, he'd offered me things rather than feeding me. He lifted the glass, which

I wished was my sippy cup, and brought it to my mouth. His hand cupped under my chin as he tilted the glass and fed me small sips of apple juice. His gaze was back on mine and the world could have gone up in flames around us and I wouldn't have noticed.

The blue of his eyes was like the sky on a bright day when a plane travels about the clouds. I wanted to fly right into the depth of them and never return. What had been a damn awful day had become this... *amazingness.*

What I'd suspected about this man wasn't close to how caring he was being towards me, despite the audience. Past hurts inflicted by those who'd seen me as nothing more than a plaything to trifle with faded into nothingness while I felt the rough pads of his fingertips catch the drips from my lower lip.

A moment later, the finger went to his mouth and a moan slid out as he sucked the drip of juice.

The cough from the opposite side of the table brought me back to reality with a hard thump. Blushing at the openly staring men, I dipped my chin, back to feeling uncertain at what my expression might have revealed.

"So, want to tell me what you were playing at, Austin?"

I wanted to thank Weston for taking the focus off me, so I pressed my hand on his thigh without thinking and squeezed gently.

The leg beneath my palm flexed under the material and before I could consider if I should move away, he covered mine and the rough pad of his thumb rubbed circles over the skin. His gaze remained on Austin, who had slashes of red over his cheekbones.

"The situation is real. Matty explained to us that he had told you of his predicament. I thought you'd be best person to deal with this, *having a personal stake in the outcome*." Something passed between the two men and I felt they were having some kind of silent conversation that Gaines and I weren't party to.

Then it struck what Austin had said. Personal stake? Did he mean *me*?

Had Weston told him about me?

I couldn't see how, when Weston said he'd only figured out Peter connected me to Austin this evening.

Weston never stopped tracing patterns over the back of my hand and I sighed dreamily at the attention. Attention that showed me I wasn't being ignored while he spoke to Austin.

"I do, though it would have been nice to have given me a heads up that you knew Matty and I were acquainted."

Austin's grin was sheepish, but he shrugged. "And what fun would that have been?" He pointed between the two of us. "You might have also said no, and then Matty wouldn't be smiling like he is after having another run in with Peter today."

I'd discovered that when the man beside me looked at me, he made me feel like nothing else mattered. When he twisted his head in my direction, my heart lodged itself against the wall of my chest and refused to budge. All I could see was concern and it left me breathless, my ears buzzing loudly.

His lips moved and for a second, I couldn't make out what Weston was saying. His free hand brushed at the side of my face, pushing back the silky strands of hair before warm fingers slipped around the back of my neck and cupped it.

A shiver of desire came hot on its heels when those fingers squeezed gently, making me feel the weight of protectiveness in the clasp. "Tell me what happened?"

"He just got into my face and wouldn't get that I didn't want to talk to him. We were with a bunch of work colleagues and I didn't want to attract any more attention, so I didn't leave and give him a piece of my mind, like I wanted to. He's being an A-hole."

The latter came out more as a sob at the memory of how awful Peter had gotten. I didn't get what his problem was, and it was becoming intolerable, to the point I was considering if I needed to find another job. A part of me contemplated this was exactly what Peter wanted, but I wasn't sure how much more I could take, and I said as much.

Weston growled and set the hairs on my arms to lift. "He's not going to chase you out. It has to be a decision you make because a better job has come along."

Gaines was nodding, his eyes glistening with tears. "Has he been doing this the entire time since he cheated, and you dumped him?"

"No..." I stopped to consider Gaines' question more seriously when I recalled some of the tricky situations Peter had caused over the past year. "Or not to the same level. He was being dickish after I said it was over. I couldn't see why, when he was still with Richard, so I put it down to the fact I'd dumped him before he could do it to me."

I looked at Weston, who continued to keep hold of me, the gentle touch giving me strength and settling a gamut of uneasy feelings that wanted to take over. "You know, like I've injured his pride, even though he was the one who was the cheater."

Had I inadvertently created this situation by dumping him?

No one spoke initially while Austin wore a frown, his fingers drumming on the table next to his empty plate. "There has to be a trigger if he's escalating his behavior."

"I haven't done anything, I swear."

Weston turned the palm on my leg over and threaded his fingers with mine. "Then we'll work to figure out what the problem is and make sure Peter sees sense." His voice was soft and the exact opposite of the determined set of his jaw.

"How?" I asked, a quiver in my voice that had nothing to do with fear and everything to do with how this man set off little explosives of need inside me, looking the way he did... for me. "And what if he doesn't... see sense?"

"He will." This came from Austin and Gaines grinned at his Daddy while Weston tilted his head as if in full agreement.

Oh!

Chapter Seven

Weston

I had some thoughts about why Peter was escalating his behavior towards Matty. The time I'd spent looking through his social media gave me some indications things were not as they seemed between Peter and Richard. With no factual evidence, I wasn't going to speculate on that for now. Matty was distressed enough without me adding to it.

As for the rest of the evening, it was an unexpected pleasure, and it was hard to consider leaving when Austin stood wearing an expectant look. "Are you ready for me to drop you back to your car?"

The hand entwined with mine clutched a little tighter and I glanced at the darkness outside, figuring out my options. "Can you give me ten minutes? I'd like to speak with Pumpkin alone."

Gaines jumped up and took hold of Austin's sleeve, tugging him eagerly out of the kitchen with both men wearing equally enormous grins. "Come on Daddy, I need to check to see if I can find a cup like Matty's." I could hear Gaines giggling as they disappeared.

I shook my head and turned more towards Matty, who was using a fingertip to rub at a spot on the table, his gaze fixed on what he was doing. Reaching for the hand, I held both and encouraged him to look at me. "Pumpkin, can you look at me, please?" I phrased it as a question, using my Daddy voice.

His head popped up and long eyelashes lowered, shielding his eyes.

I breathed in his floral scent, my pulse getting a swift boost. "These last few weeks where we've been meeting in the park... at a regular time, do you want to continue with *just* doing that?"

He blinked rapidly, meeting my gaze. I could see from the confused look he wore that there was a lot going on inside his head.

"What... we... this..." He let go of my hand to raise it between us, then let it flop into his lap as if unsure of what he wanted to say.

"What I'm asking is, do you want to date me? Do more with me than what we've been doing on Saturday's in the park," I clarified, realizing I wasn't being clear enough for him.

What appeared to be relief came as he sagged and grinned at me. "Yes, as..." his smile dimmed as he brought up his free hand and chewed on his thumbnail, once more looking down. The awkwardness was something new and my Daddy side wanted to remove it for him immediately.

"Do you want to know if I'm a Daddy?" His head was bobbing before I could continue. "I hoped what I did through dinner time would have made it clear. I am a Daddy. And I'm sorry, I shouldn't jump to conclusions."

A shy smile came with an adorable blush. "Do you like Littles?"

"Yes." I came forward until our mouths were close enough I could feel his breath on my lips as it stuttered out of him. "I also like boys who wear cute fox outfits, too."

The smile that reached his eyes was like the sun rising over an ocean, highlighting sparkling waves with thousands of diamonds scattered in them. Beautiful and tempting, it stole my breath, encouraging me to bridge the small gap between us and kiss him.

Watching for any signs he didn't want it, I lingered. My free hand slid around the back of his neck, fingers sinking into the silky strands of his hair, caressing them before moving to allow for our lips to touch lightly. Just the barest of touches. His body shuddered, his breathing uneven.

Once, twice, I pressed my lips to his until his body melted into mine. I changed the angle, feeling the contours of his mouth against mine. Exploring the warm softness and witnessing how he went pliant against me.

His scent was all I could smell as he pressed his chest to mine. A whimper came from the parting lips as I sank into the taste of him. The garlic from dinner lingered, yet beneath it was a pure sweetness that was entirely Matty. Addictive. One kiss wasn't enough to feed my hunger. My chest tightened and burned with the need to breathe, yet I didn't want to stop. How could I when he whimpered and moaned so delightfully each time I changed the angle to enjoy his reactions? I found an angle that made him quiver and his hands move to clutch at my button-down.

He was all but sitting on me in a very awkward position when I eased back, gasping for breath. A deep flush covered his cheeks and his heavy-lidded eyes made my dick twitch and thicken further with desire.

"Beautiful," I murmured and cupped both his cheeks, giving into the temptation to kiss him again. He encouraged me to deepen it with greedy moans but I reluctantly forced myself to resist, unsure how much time had passed, and positive Austin would be back sooner rather than later. It didn't hurt my ego when Matty chased my lips as if he couldn't bear for me to stop.

I kissed the tip of his nose. "Pumpkin, you are a temptation."

"Is that a bad thing?" he asked in a breathless voice that held excitement, judging by the sparkle in his eyes and how his body squirmed against me.

My gaze dropped to his obvious arousal, pressing against the front of his slacks. The sight didn't help me with the taste of him lingering on my tongue. "It is when Austin will be back any minute and we haven't discussed when I can next come and see you."

He sucked his bottom lip between his teeth and his nose wrinkled. It popped out a second later. "Anytime you want," he said in such a rush, it sounded like one long word.

I chuckled and eased him back onto the bench, needing a little breathing room from his eagerness, scent, and taste, which all tempted me to throw him over my shoulder and ask where his room was. That was not how I did things, or it hadn't been until I got tempted by the sweet smiling boy in front of me. "How about tomorrow..." I suddenly realized that I'd promised to meet Saul at the gym the following evening to do a training session. As I'd already set the date,

I cursed internally, not wanting to be that person who would change his plans for a date... unless.

"I've planned to help a friend out with a training program. Do you want to come and join us? We can go out to dinner afterwards."

A little furrow appeared between his blond brows. "Would your friend come to dinner too?" A quick shake of my head removed the furrow. "Okay, I'll come. I'm sure it'll be fun."

~/~/~/~

The day had dragged on. The only bright spots were the messages Matty had sent after we'd exchanged numbers the night before, getting one more kiss at the door before I left with Austin. I'd also gained a promise that if Peter was to hassle him, that he was to message me. I'd done a deeper dive into Peter's life and I'd need to talk to Matty about that when we were alone.

Last night, Austin had hardly shut the car door before he had jumped on my intentions, wanting to know what I wanted from Matty. What had started as a chance meeting had progressed to something more. I had feelings for Matty, which had developed over the last couple of months. If he wanted a full time Daddy, I desired to be it. Austin had been very clear I wasn't to mess Matty around after explaining his past record with dating.

The warning was entirely unnecessary though, I'd not do anything to hurt Matty intentionally. I'd become invested in his happiness after the second time I'd met him—okay, the moment I laid eyes on him—and he brought out my protective side. Last night had upped those protective urges, getting time to see Matty be himself.

"Will you quit looking at the door. I thought you were here to help me?" Saul groused, running a hand through his hair as he stepped in front of me, bringing my attention back to him.

"Shit, sorry." I checked my watch. "It's just I don't want Matty walking in here and feeling out of place." Matty hadn't asked anything about where the training was taking place, and I'd not considered if he'd feel uncomfortable inside the gym I was a member of. There was a gym in my apartment building, only it was more for those who just wanted to do simple exercise to keep generally fit, nothing to the level that required daily commitment and hours of work.

I glanced about. Everywhere I looked, large, muscled men worked out, grunting and groaning while lifting weights that probably weighed more than Matty did. There were men doing strength training, showing off their skills to anyone paying attention.

Gaines clearly had a level of fitness to perform on a pole and do the aerial work Austin had bragged his boy could do. That had to mean Matty exercised too? He was as slim as Gaines and from what I'd felt, his muscle tone was good.

"You've zoned out on me again. Is it even worth you being here?"

Shit!

I gave him an apologetic smile. "I'm nervous." The second I said it, I realized it was the truth. In the gym, they knew me as a beast and I didn't want to scare Matty off, not when we had just agreed to date.

"You?" Saul scoffed, then frowned, stepping nearer to look at me more closely. "You are nervous!" he exclaimed, loud enough that the clanging of the weights hitting the stand next to us didn't block it out.

"Yes," I hissed, glancing at the two guys now eyeing us with more interest than before, "and I'd prefer you didn't tell everyone."

His lips quivered as he nodded, eyes gleaming with amusement under the lights as he slapped my bare shoulder. "You'll be fine. Just show him how strong you are and he'll not be thinking 'bout anything else. In fact, I'd bet a year's wages on that."

The door opened, drawing my attention. Matty's blond head poked around it and I didn't miss his eyes widening or him losing the color from his cheeks. A guy coming up behind him left him no option but to step inside. I waved at him, hoping it would remove the look of... *trepidation?*

Was this a mistake?

I got a sinking feeling in the pit of my stomach as his nose wrinkled in what appeared to be distaste as I thread my way through the equipment with Saul right behind me, muttering, "Fuck, he's sweet. He could give me a toothache any time."

He was sweet and looked totally out of place, dressed as he was. The skinny sweat pants in bright yellow had a matching zip up jacket. Neither looked practical for working out in. His sneakers were bright orange and flashed lights as he hesitantly came to me.

I didn't stop walking as I answered, only loud enough for Saul to hear, "He's taken and you have a boyfriend."

I amped up my smile as I reached for Matty and took hold of his hand, uncaring about who was watching. Never one to hide that I was gay now I was out of the army, I bent quite a way to reach him so I could give his startled mouth a kiss.

His lips remained open as he stared up at me wide eyed. When I released his mouth, his gaze dipped down my body. A look that resembled that of a tiger who hadn't eaten for weeks, and had spotted fresh meat, appeared on Matty's face.

Having dressed to train, I'd not considered the small shorts that revealed most of my thighs or fitted wife beater that hugged my muscular chest were anything more than practical. Matty's expression said differently and eased a little of my nerves. "See something interesting, Pumpkin?"

"You look hot," he answered, then clamped his lips together and rolled his eyes to the ceiling.

Saul shoved me aside and held out his hand. "Seems as Wes has forgotten his manners, I'm Saul. I work with Wes and Austin. You're friends with Gaines, right?"

He nodded and took the hand Saul offered. "I'm Matty. Gaines is my best friend, and it's nice to meet you, Saul." He glanced about. His gaze jumped from one thing to another, not lingering for more than a second. "Isn't the training you're doing running? I don't think you'll have space in here."

Saul's deep laughter competed with the noises in the gym. "Hell, no. I ain't no runner. Your boy over there," he jabbed his thumb in my direction, "he's the best trainer when it comes to strength and agility."

"He is?" Matty regarded me once more with interest that made blood surge to places it had no business going in a busy gym.

Chapter Eight

Matty

Whatever I'd considered was going to happen when I met Weston, it wasn't... this. I'd figured training meant running. That was how I'd assumed Weston kept fit. This overly macho gym where the men looked like they were training for the world's strongest man competition was nowhere near what I thought was going to be happening.

I did not exercise.

This was hardcore, and the sight of all Weston's rippling muscles under the skimpy outfit proved he did this regularly.

"You okay?" he asked, looking concerned, which he should be!

I was in a gym, and it seemed my new boyfriend was some sort of expert physical trainer. "Erm... you aren't expecting me to take part, are you?"

Saul's chuckle stopped abruptly as Weston threw a hard look at him before returning his attention to me. "Don't you like exercising?"

How to answer that?

I glanced at the men who clearly enjoyed what they were doing despite the grunts and groans they made. "On what scale?" I asked carefully.

It was his turn to chuckle as he grinned at me. "I didn't know there was a scale, Pumpkin."

I nodded eagerly. "Oh yes, there is." I took a depth breath and went with the truth. "One is where walking is good for you, so it can be fun as long as it's not too far. Ten is where you do things to make your body hurt." I shook my head, stressing the point as I whirled a finger up in the air. "This place is clearly a ten."

"Oh gods," Saul snorted and laughed in earnest, making me worry when he bent at the waist, looking like he was struggling for breath.

I mean, I think I'm funny, but he was taking it way too far.

Weston didn't take his eyes off me and though the smile remained attached to his lips, the lines deepened around his eyes, showing he might be more amused than he was letting on. "Do you do any exercise... besides walking," he said in a hurry, clearly able to tell that I was about to point out walking was exercise.

I chewed on my lower lip, tilting my head to the side as I considered what he might class as exercise. In the end, I gave up and shrugged. He needed to know now that I would never be like the men I could see around me. "No…" I came forward and whispered, "it's cruel to punish your body until your muscles rebel and tell you off." I gave an exaggerated shudder, though it was only part put on.

"It's cruel…" he spluttered and appeared to struggle to hold back his laughter.

Saul wasn't in much better shape. His body now shook with laughter and he was drawing attention from some weightlifters within ear shot.

Had I made a huge mistake by coming inside after seeing what kind of place this was? "Why yes, cruel. Have you seen those people that make all those noises 'cause their body hates them after deciding to punish it? I've seen what it does to those folks silly enough to want Gaines to teach them to use the poll." For emphasis, I shook my head. "That's not for me. I like all my limbs to function all the time without wanting to cry when I move."

A couple of men working out with heavy weights continued to take an interest in the conversation, so I smiled politely at them. I wasn't talking about them, more myself, and I hoped they realized that. I mean, I really didn't want to cause a problem and have one of them decide I was being insulting.

Weston's smile returned and sent shivers through me with how he got a gleam in his eyes that suggested I wasn't going to like his next suggestion. "Maybe I could change your mind with a game of ball?"

A choked sound came from Saul before I could find my voice to reply and Weston gave him another hard look, before grinning at me as he slipped his arm through mine. "Let's go over to the floor mats."

Weston's masculine scent increased as he drew me to him and blocked out the smells of sweaty men. I wanted to protest, although how bad could a game of ball be? I enjoyed playing ball.

Not that I thought Weston was talking about the ones I was interested in. They came with lots of naked skin.

Steered through the large room, I noted the floor to ceiling mirrors at both ends.

Was that so no one could miss when you made a fool of yourself?

They staggered workout benches with huge weight sets throughout the center of the room. There was a row of exercise equipment, recumbent bikes, treadmills, and cross fit machines sitting down at the far end of the large space. All occupied by sweating individuals—idiots.

At an empty padded black bench tucked in the room's corner, near what appeared to be a section of hanging bars, Weston encouraged me to sit. When I had, he crouched in front of me, blocking out the rest of the room. "I'm going to get Saul sorted with a routine. You can watch and see if there is anything besides playing ball you'd like to try with Daddy."

He sounded so confident that I would. I didn't have the heart to say 'yeah, in your dreams' so instead I nodded, letting how he'd called himself Daddy settle my nerves. Seeing the distance between us and those working out, I gave in to my need to answer in kind. "Okay, Daddy."

A kiss to my forehead after brushing back my bangs gave me a boost, much like the vitamin shots that Austin insisted I drink with Gaines. Weston's eyes twinkled as he bounced up to spin around and head to where Saul was.

I bit my bottom lip to stop the groan from escaping at the ass now facing me. The shorts hid nothing. That high, tight ass was the thing of dreams. I might not like exercise, but from this vantage point, I could sure appreciate it for what it was worth. The muscles flexed and rippled as came to a stop in front of Saul who was holding a large black ball. Was he wanting me to play ball with that?

It looked big and heavy from the way Saul's biceps expanded out of his T-shirt. Was this a trick way to get me to exercise, too? A frown marred my brow as I strained to hear their conversation, my gaze narrowing on them. The overall noise in the place made it impossible to hear anything this far away.

Although the room was full of men with varying degrees of body size and some wearing less than Weston, none of them pulled my attention the same way Weston did. He wore a focused look that was much the same as it had been the day before, when he'd taken care of me at the dinner table. His confidence was something else and it kind of oozed out of him. I could see it as he took the ball and made several interesting moves I didn't understand.

When he put it down by his sneakered foot, the smile—which was all mischief—he directed at me made my mouth dry. He gave me a thumbs up and next thing he was on the mats doing some interesting stretches. Mesmerized, my gaze never moved as I assumed what he was doing was to make sure he didn't hurt himself. My gaze lingered on well-defined legs and abs as he lunged and stretched his arms to the ceiling, calling out instructions to Saul.

Having been worried I might get bored, that idea quickly evaporated. There was no chance of that with how much fun it was to watch Weston put Saul through his paces. An air of authority exuded from him and made others pay attention. If I'd not known he had a military background, I would have guessed he'd been in the services by how he came across. There was something strong and dependable about him. He used humor and a stern voice that made me squirm a time or two to get Saul to do what he wanted. It didn't take long before both men gleamed with sweat under the industrial lights.

Sometime later, Weston returned to the ball he'd held earlier, after wiping his hands on a towel he'd thrown on an empty bench beside me. He walked over to the hanging bars that were closest to a wall. I shifted forward when he put the ball between his sneakers and looked up. When he jumped to grip onto the metal bar, Saul moved into my line of sight, so I shifted down the bench and then lost any brain function I might have had at him hanging from the bars. Every muscle strained in his upper body. He gave me a saucy wink then threw the ball at the wall with his feet and caught it between his sneakers on its return. If that wasn't impressive enough, next he threw the ball over the bar he was hanging from, only to catch it once more between his feet.

I gawped and possibly drooled, heat flooding my entire body.

His vest rode up to reveal cum gutters and a wall of muscle I never considered would be under Weston's clothes. The room seemed to get impossibly hot, as if the thermostat had gone on the blink and got stuck on high. I never took my gaze off the man who made it seem so easy to play ball this way. It wasn't. I didn't need to be an expert to understand what he was doing took genuine effort and commitment. My comment earlier about Weston being hot, yeah, this was unearthly heat. Incendiary.

I lost count of how many times the ball hit the wall and he threw over the bar above his head and caught it with just his feet, but his hair was dripping with sweat and his shorts were clingier than they had been as he dropped to the ground. There were several cheers and some clapping as he picked up the ball, which he offered to Saul.

He twisted, bowed, then grinned before returning his attention to Saul.

Saul, I could see, took longer to get his rhythm and was much slower. There was no ease of rotation between the ball hitting the wall and going over the bar above his head. The effortless transition between the throwing and catching was gone.

Throwing and catching!

Oh... oh no... did he think...

My thoughts were stuttering as much as my heart as I eyed the man instructing Saul. Was this the ball game he expected me to play? No... he couldn't think... *I was going to do this?*

Saliva deserted my mouth as I met his stare, and he grinned so wide it was as if the corners of his lips were trying to say hello to his ears. I shook my head with a conscious effort. Because I needed to be clear, there was no way I was going to hang from that bar and throw a ball at a wall. Not in this lifetime. Heck, not in any lifetime!

Thirty minutes later, a way too smiley Saul, who was dripping all over the mat on the floor, gave us a salute and headed off toward a door I assumed was the locker room. The towel Weston had been using periodically to wipe the sweat off his face and hands hung around his neck when he came to where I'd decided my butt was staying planted. It was the only safe place to be.

"You wanna play ball with me, Pumpkin?" I shook my head as emphatically as I could manage. "Are you sure you don't want to help Daddy get a proper workout?" He crouched in front of me on legs that should have been like two strings of spaghetti after the workout he'd given Saul and himself.

Wasn't what he'd just done a proper workout?

The horror that my question could get a 'no' left me speechless while he gently tucked a couple of curls behind my ear, giving me a wicked smile that went straight to a part of my anatomy that was so not in charge right then. "You could hang off Daddy while I throw the ball. Give me a little bit more of a challenge. Wouldn't you like to help Daddy?"

The way he phrased it suggested I had a choice, but my brain had latched on to actually hanging off him and where the *balls*—not the one at his feet—would be in relation to mine.

"How does that work?" I asked when my tongue got with the programme. My dick had run straight ahead of us.

He rose and wiped his face and neck, then tossed the towel next to me, offering me a hand. The second his fingers clasped mine, it registered why he had so many calluses on the palm of his hands.

Leading me to the hanging bar, he released my hand to put the ball between his sneakers. "Come here, Pumpkin." He crouched and took my hands and placed them around his neck. "When I lift you, tuck your legs around my middle and cross your ankles so you get a good hold of me."

With a nod, his hands came under my armpits and he lifted me. My fingers clung on to the back of his damp neck as I wrapped my legs around his middle. He smelled of musk and hints of his aftershave. His clothes were damp and I was sure they would leave a stain on my tracksuit.

Did I care?

Nope!

I knew I wasn't big, but wrapped around Weston, it brought home just how much buffer and larger than me he was. My groin pressed against his abs and I realized the error of my ways when he jumped up and the rippling muscles rubbed against a part of me that thought we had started party time.

Many emotions ran through me at the show of strength, but I couldn't focus on those when he pressed himself so tightly against me. I hid my warming face, burying it in the side of Weston's neck as I groaned.

He hung suspended for a few moments and I felt more than heard his chuckle. "Hold tight, Pumpkin."

That was all the warning he gave me. I heard the ball hit the wall, a whoosh of air as we swung to catch it. Weston's muscles bunched and moved as his legs lifted and his groin cupped my backside, rubbing. A moan ghosted over Weston's neck as his cock thickened against my clenching ass. Then we were moving again as he caught the ball between his feet.

Why wasn't this kind of physical sport offered by gyms? This I'd have paid good cash for.

Each rub and swing sent zinging pleasure through me. Those around us faded into obscurity as the whole of my attention zeroed in on the man I clung to. Sweat soaked my clothes and I knew Gaines would be seriously concerned for my wellbeing at allowing an exercising, sweaty person to touch me.

I caught our reflection in the mirrors and my mouth dropped open at the sexy visual. The feeling of him under me was amazing but seeing his fluid moves was... spectacular. There wasn't an inch of him that wasn't working to keep us hanging from the bars while he repeatedly threw the ball and caught it.

Puffs of breath gusted over the side of my face as he dropped the ball and it rolled to the crowd we'd gathered. With ease, he dropped to the floor. The jerk got me tightening my legs around him. I couldn't disguise my arousal with how a deep need made me achingly hard. His body shielded me from those closest to us, for now.

Please don't put me down! I silently begged.

"Did you enjoy that?" A twinkle in his blue eyes said he was fully aware of how much I'd enjoyed myself.

"Is this a new training method?" someone called out from behind me, giving me time to work on getting my body to behave.

"Wanna try it with big Mike?" Weston called back, looking over my head.

"Fuck, man, I'd never be able to jump with that big buffoon on me. Maybe I can use your sunflower?"

"In your dreams. This is my boy. Go find your own." As if to prove his point, he effortlessly shifted me onto his hip, keeping me close.

None of the guys I'd dated in the past had ever moved me with such little effort. But it was the possessive tone and how he looked at me that registered he was taking care no one witnessed my reaction to him.

He's concealing me!

Any resistance I might have had—none, I'd none—would have fled at his protective behavior. Back at the bench, he placed me down, keeping up the comradery with some guys in the room as he plucked the towel off the bench and placed it in my lap.

When the men left to continue with their workouts, he winked at me. "Next time, I think I'll need to exercise *with you in private*." He pretended to cough. "We wouldn't want to give everyone something else to be jealous of."

Exercise like this I could totally get on board with!

Chapter Nine

Weston

The stack of papers relating to Peter on my home office desk had grown considerably over the last few days. I'd had to reach out to Warner to have my work schedule changed so I could do more surveillance on Peter.

Matty had messaged me several times to alert me to Peter's continuing harassment of him. What I'd discovered was that the guy was a total creep. And I was aware I wasn't as unbiased as I should have been, but Peter was a spoiled asshole who didn't like it when he didn't get what he wanted, from what I could ascertain. His escalating behavior towards Matty pointed more and more to the fact his relationship with his new beau wasn't as happy as portrayed on the surface. From what I had gathered, Peter inadvertently getting caught cheating had brought about his own demise with Matty and forced his hand with Richard.

A few of Peter's colleagues and friends I'd got to speak to suggested Peter hadn't wanted to lose face when Matty had dumped him and he got stuck with Richard. How they'd gotten to the engagement stage didn't matter. What did was how to stop the asshole from taking out his frustrations on Matty.

Checking the time, I rose from my desk to get changed out of my sweats. It was Friday and I planned on surprising Matty with an evening out with a unique experience. He loved to be creative, and he talked enthusiastically about his marketing designs. On a web search, I'd found a place in West Humboldt Park that did street graffiti art workshops. Matty could learn assorted styles and techniques from guest artists and could get creative on canvas, which he could bring home at the end of class. It sounded fun, so I booked it and made a snack box for us both, which the website suggested doing as they didn't offer food.

I was excited to see his reaction to what I'd planned. Dressed in old, ripped jeans, a college sweater and a leather jacket, I shoved my wallet into my back pocket, checking I had my cell phone for the e-tickets. Collecting my keys and a loaded bag, which I threw over my shoulder, I headed out of the door.

The nights were drawing in, so it was getting dark when I pulled up outside Matty's building and parked in a spot that allowed me to see the main exit. It was still early, so I sat listening to Radio Chicago, my fingers tapping on the steering wheel, a wide grin firmly fixed to my face at the prospect of spending another evening with Matty.

After our workout at the gym, it had been a genuine struggle to keep things light and easy with him. I'd quickly seen the horror at the idea I'd make him do a workout, so I'd opted for fun. But it had backfired when one particular muscle hadn't gotten as exhausted with the workout as the rest of me. A starry-eyed Matty was a hard one to resist, especially when he'd looked at me that way.

At the memory, my cock stirred and I shifted my thoughts away from territory that wouldn't help me in my campaign in developing a strong bond with a man I had fallen for very fast. There was nothing about him that didn't intrigue me and keep me on my toes. He was perfect, if there was such a thing.

The night before, when I'd once more gone to Gaines' home for dinner—this time with an invite—I'd got to experience Matty's Little side. Fuck, he was so damn cute when he was playful. He had this adorable expression when he wanted me to do something for him. He'd tilt his head to the side and tug on one of his curls while looking up at me shyly from under his eyelashes. It was a move I would never be able to resist—not that I'd have any intention of doing so.

Movement in front of me brought my attention to the man who rushed out the main door. My gaze narrowed on Peter, who was alone. He walked off towards the side of the building in the direction I'd first watched Matty head to go home. *What was he up to? Was he trying to accost Matty on his way home?*

Out of the car before I registered my intention, I went straight for the main door, intending to reach Matty before Peter did. Barely a moment later, people poured out of the building like ants. I stood off to the side, watchful for Matty, then cursed as a tall dude stood in front of me and paused, reaching into his pocket for his ringing phone. It was all the time Peter needed, as I missed Matty exiting behind the man.

The second I caught Matty's retreating form, I darted after him, glaring at Peter when he stepped directly into Matty's path.

No.

No.

Fucking hell, no.

Taking determined steps, Peter's focus was solely on Matty as I heard him say, "What have you been saying, you little shit?"

My arm slipped around Matty's shoulder. His whole body froze before his head flicked in my direction. His gaze met mine and the relief was palpable as he sagged against me, his lips forming into a beautiful big grin. "Daddy."

Glad I'd interceded before Peter had the chance to start on Matty, I cast my gaze to Peter, giving him a withering look. "I don't think we've met." The smile I offered was more feral than friendly. "I'm Weston, *Matty's Daddy.*" I didn't offer my hand as I held his stare, firing warnings at him he'd better heed if he didn't want to find his face rearranged.

If the air could have crackled with tension, I was positive it would have. Peter appeared to struggle with what to say in my presence when his gaze swept over me. His lips moved and he wore an expression much like he was eating something very unpleasant. "I want a *private word* with Matty, if you don't mind," he finally snapped, like I was some naughty child to reprimand.

What had Matty seen in this dick?

Matty shifted closer to me, and I tightened my hold, offering him silent reassurance everything was going to be okay. "Pumpkin and I don't have any secrets from each other. Whatever you have to say to him, you can discuss in front of me." I smiled sweetly at Matty. "Isn't that right, Pumpkin?"

"Yes, Daddy." He snuggled right in, his smile as bright as a star. He looped an arm around me, his fingers tugging on my leather belt. His flowery scent was all I could smell as I inhaled. "*We* don't have any secrets from each other." He aimed the barbed comment at Peter.

"So, what did you want to discuss? Before we address how you spoke to my boy?"

The lights coming from the building made it easy to see the flush darkening Peter's tanned cheeks. A second later, he stood a little straighter, bristling, wearing a scowl that made him look as threatening as Scooby Doo. Although I gave him credit for continuing to hold eye contact with me.

"Yes?" I prompted when he didn't seem inclined to say more.

Peter aimed the scowl at Matty. "We will discuss this on *Monday. In private.*"

At the stress he put on those words and the way Matty flinched at the threat, I weighed my words carefully. Before moving, I kissed the top of Matty's head, encouraging him to let go of me, then stepped between Matty and Peter.

Voices and laughter carried from those happy to be leaving work. I ignored them, keeping my focus on the man in front of me. "I believe you weren't listening to me." My tone could have cut through sheet metal with the heat of my anger. "If you wish to talk to Pumpkin, then you will do it in front of me. You won't like the consequences if you choose to disregard what I'm saying. You will only address him inside this building if it is work related. Are we clear?"

"You can't tell me what I can or can't do," he blustered, going an unhealthy shade of red.

My sneakers hit the toes of his shoes as I stepped into his body, towering over him, using my height advantage to make him crane his head back to keep looking at me. "You really don't want to push me on this," I growled menacingly, ensuring he got the full force of my anger. "I'm not some soft-hearted boy you can push around. You so much as look at Matty sideways, or even breathe near him, I will bring a universe of hurt down on you. *Am I making myself clear?*"

He took a step back and I witnessed the fear his eyes could not hide. Happy I'd made my point, I swung around and went to a wide eyed Matty.

He leapt at me before I'd come to a stop, the bag he was carrying banging off my thigh as he wrapped his arms around my body and buried his face in my chest.

Stroking a hand over his silky curls, I cupped the back of his neck, feeling the shivers running through him. Was he upset? Cold? Both? "You okay, Pumpkin?" I kept my voice low, so it didn't carry when I heard shoes slapping on the concrete.

"Thank you," he whispered, just loud enough for me to hear.

Once more, I brushed my lips over his silky curls, bringing him a little closer. A snuffling sound followed, and I chuckled as I realized he was smelling me. "Anytime, Pumpkin," I answered softly. I meant it. Peter would not get any more chances to fuck with Matty.

Peter was going to find out just how protective I was of Matty if he continued to push. I made a mental note to have a word with Austin about this run in. It wasn't—or it hadn't been—part of the plan to confront the asshole in this way. My protective Daddy side didn't care about plans, only Matty.

The arms hugging me a little tighter got my thoughts shifting to what was important right then—leaving to go have some fun. Only I lingered for a few more seconds, loving how his small frame fit in my arms, before I felt him shiver.

I guided him to the car and buckled him into the seat wordlessly, giving him a kiss when he puckered up. His lips were soft and plump, tasting sweet, suggesting not long before he'd eaten something that wasn't healthy. I didn't sigh, though I wanted to when I recalled Austin had joked about Matty's sweet tooth. It was a conversation for another day, as tonight was about spoiling Matty.

It didn't take long to merge with the traffic. I had to concentrate, but I felt the weight of Matty's stare in the dark interior of the car. "What, Pumpkin?"

"When you said you'd hurt Peter... what did you mean by that?"

It was curiosity I heard rather than fright, so I answered truthfully. "There are many points on the body that, if you apply pressure, can cause untold pain but leave no trace behind." I flashed a grin at Matty that spoke to how much harm I'd inflict on Peter if he continued to torment my boy, before looking back at the traffic in front of me.

There was a pause, long enough to get me to bring my gaze back to Matty when the traffic slowed. My breath caught in my throat for the split second as I witnessed his angelic smile. "I know it's wrong to tell fibs, but I gotta say, Daddy, I'm tempted to fib just to give Peter a taste of his own medicine."

Laughter burst out of me as I slowed, looking for the next turning I needed to take. I couldn't argue with his need to get back at Peter after what he'd explained the man had been doing, *but still*.

That didn't mean if Peter stepped out of line again, that we'd be meeting on friendly terms. Fuck no, then all bets were off.

Chapter Ten

Matty

Holding Weston's hand, I glanced at the buildings we passed while hurrying to get out of the wind driving down the street. My jacket didn't offer any resistance against the chill. In trying to make myself feel better this morning, I'd chosen unwisely. Weston let go of my hand and slipped an arm around my shivering shoulders and hugged me into the warmth of his body. Taking a deep inhale, the scent of pine and something fresh and masculine came from him.

My gaze went back to the busy street while I tried to figure out what his plans for the evening were. He'd been very cryptic the day before, only advising me to bring some clothes that I didn't mind getting dirty. His pace slowed and I looked up at the building in front of us, still none the wiser.

It was easier to think about what we were doing now than what had happened with putrid Peter.

Does it make me a bad person to want Daddy to smack Peter in the mouth?

I'd only been half joking when I suggested Weston should hurt Peter. The man was insufferable and appeared to be there every time I turned around at work. It was making me jumpy and I was struggling to keep my focus, which hadn't gone unnoticed by my boss.

A calloused finger ran down my forehead and I realized we'd come to a stop at a door. "Why the frown, Pumpkin?"

Positive the smile I gave him didn't reach my eyes, I shielded them with my eyelashes and shrugged off his concern. "I'm just trying to figure out what we're doing—"

The same finger went to my lips and pressed gently against them and Weston shook his head, stopping me from elaborating further.

The wind caught the top silver strands of his hair and blew them around in a messy style that didn't detract from how attractive he was. "No, Pumpkin. Don't try to fob me off. I can see something is bothering you. You need to tell Daddy what it is so he can fix it."

My sigh was long and loud, making his lips twitch, but he held my stare, encouraging me to tell the truth. "I wasn't joking about you hurting putrid Peter. Does that make me a bad person?"

"No, it makes you an honest one." His gaze hardened and a shiver ran up my spine. "Has Peter ever hurt you physically?" The deep timbre of his voice held a steely quality to it.

"No, other than snatching my fox ears and breaking them, he just gets in my face and gets all aggressive. Like he did tonight," I stated quickly, to reassure Weston while I watched him closely. A glint appeared in his crystal blue eyes that turned them icy.

"Good." Nothing about how he said the word suggested it was.

A couple of men interrupted our conversation as they stopped behind us. Both were of a similar height and build, wearing casual clothes. The blond guy offered a smile and asked, "Is this the place for the graffiti art class, do you know?"

"A graffiti art class," I asked excitedly, our conversation forgotten about with the possibility of the date. "Is that what we're doing?"

"Yes," Weston said to me and then nodded at the two men, who grinned at me as I squealed in delight. "It is." Weston reached for the door and stepped aside to let the guys go in front of us.

Inside, I babbled excitedly on the lift ride. By the time we were in the studio, my excitement levels were at an all-time high. The scent of spray paint and the bold-colored artwork hanging on one wall made me giddy.

"Daddy, look," I dragged Weston to where a large canvas sat with what, to me, looked like a rainbow of books going towards the moon, which was also full of color, unaware of our audience. "See here," I pointed to the right side of the canvas, "it's like they've created a stairway to the sky," I enthused in the room's silence.

It took a moment for the quietness to register as I glanced away from the artwork, to the other nine people scattered around the room. It felt way smaller with them all staring at me, with varying degrees of curiosity.

I ran through what I'd said, and I swung to look at Weston in alarm, an apology forming on my lips for calling him Daddy in public.

His grin and unconcerned demeanor eased the ants that had evacuated their ant hill and were all marching through my belly.

"It does, Pumpkin." His smile widened, and he chuckled. "Let's hope I'm not about to make a fool of myself with my stick painted people," he said, breaking the tension further.

"L.S. Lowery's work fetches lots of money," I pointed out, matching his grin. No longer the center of attention for calling Weston 'Daddy' in public, conversations restarted around us. It came so naturally, even when we'd only officially been dating a week.

It's been two months!

I giggled at the insistent voice, but considered I'd need to be more careful in the future.

Weston took his cell phone out of his pocket when a man with long dreadlocks came to us wearing a polite smile. His combat trousers were paint splattered, as was the white T-shirt, which explained why Weston had said to bring clothes that could get dirty.

"Hey, looks like you're both first timers so thanks for coming. I'm Zeke and I run these classes. If you need a place to change, there's a restroom over there." His vibe was friendly and professional as he checked out the tickets Weston had purchased.

After Weston slipped his cell phone back in his leather jacket, Zeke offered a paint stained hand to Weston first, then to me.

"I'm Matty and this is Weston." I pumped Zeke's hand enthusiastically. "What are we going to learn? Will we get to do some practice? I've always been a huge fan of graffiti art." I let go of his hand and I pointed to the piece I'd been admiring. "This is beautiful. Did you do it?"

He smiled, although he appeared a little bemused, making me realize I'd not let him answer any of my questions in my exuberance. "It is mine. Have you taken any art classes before? Not that you need to have to enjoy the evening," he quickly assured us when Weston shook his head while I nodded.

When someone called his name, Zeke glanced over at a group of three men and two women. When he returned his gaze to us, he grinned at us both. "Tonight is all about having fun. Go get changed. We'll be starting in about ten minutes, " he said, before he left to speak to the person who called his name.

There was a definite pause when Weston looked at the restroom door, then back to me. "Do you want me to help you?"

"Yes, please…" I flicked my head in both directions, checking no one was in earshot before adding, "Daddy."

"I'm fine with whatever you want to call me in public." He tweaked the end of my nose. "Unless we go to my mom's, okay? She will be accepting, but will have way too many questions no son wants to answer about his sexual preferences." His laughter was full-bodied as he looked like he was considering exactly how his mom would behave, which intrigued me. My parents would die a thousand deaths before asking about my sexual preferences.

Meeting the parents. Were we at that stage already? A little giddy at the prospect of that, I let Weston guide me to the restroom. It was empty, and I was glad so no one could fully glean what I'd meant by calling Weston Daddy. His silver hair could give them the wrong idea, though I looked nothing like Weston and the age gap, though considerable at fourteen years, wasn't enough to make him old enough to be my actual father.

I plopped my bag down on the small bench that sat in the room's corner, in front of a single row of lockers. I waited for Weston, who slipped his own bag down his arm and placed it next to mine. He opened the zip of mine and peered inside before pulling out the pale gray T-shirt that I'd shrunk in the dryer and placing it down. The soft black jersey pants that came next had lost their elasticity and bagged at the knees. I used them mainly for cleaning and thought they fit the description of what Weston suggested I needed for tonight. He laid them on the bench on top of the T-shirt. He pulled out the pair of red Crocs that had love hearts cut out down both sides, grinning at them as he dropped them to the floor. They were old and I wasn't worried about them getting stained.

He slipped off his leather jacket, and it was then I noticed what he was wearing. The black T-shirt hugged his body, revealing exactly how toned he was. Ripped jeans became faded to nearly white at the top part of his thighs, close to his groin. They had rips halfway up one thigh and at the knee of the other leg.

My fingers curled into fists to resist reaching out to stroke at the material to see if it was as soft as it looked and maybe get to touch the skin beneath.

Total badass, a younger Marlon Brando, that's how he looked to me. I swallowed three times to clear the saliva from my mouth before I could speak. "I love what you're wearing."

He glanced down, his brows drawing together before his face morphed into a sexy smirk. "Is that so?"

I nodded eagerly. "You look badass, Daddy."

His laughter erupted out of him, a sound that warmed me right down to my toes. It was vibrant and happy, making his body shake as he reached to help me out of my jacket. "Badass, love it!" he said, continuing to laugh.

His fingers nimbly undid the buttons on my shirt, exchanging it for the T-shirt. His calloused hands brushed my skin and I swallowed a moan of delight as little sparks of desire skittered through me.

When he got down on his haunches and went for the belt of my slacks, my thoughts scattered at how his tongue ran over his lower lip.

It gleamed in the overhead lights and I slammed my eyes shut when my cock thickened at the images I conjured of him running that same tongue over me.

"You doing okay, Pumpkin?" His voice was like a caress, the deep timber running over my naked skin as his fingers gently tugged my slacks down my thighs.

"Daddyyyy," I gasped at the press of one finger against the front of my boxer briefs that felt much snugger than they had mere moments ago.

The blue of his eyes darkened and danced with amusement as he tapped my left leg, getting me to lift it. He slipped off my suede boot and eased my leg out of the slacks. He repeated the move with my other leg while I practiced taking slow, shallow breaths the whole time to stop hyperventilating.

Dressed a minute later, he rose. My gaze dropped to the front of his jeans, revealing a bulge I'd felt nestled against my ass days before. One that was much bigger right now. That he had been so affected by what he'd done for me was little consolation when we were about to head out into a room full of people.

My shoulders drooped and I pouted.

A thumb traced over my lower lip and I didn't resist the temptation and sucked it right into my mouth. Giving it a solid suck, I looked at Weston from under my eyelashes as I tilted my head and tugged on a curl.

His groan sent ripples of desire through me, but it was his look of need that caused my pants to tent. He came closer as I suckled his thumb, loving the feel of the rough pad sliding over my tongue. "Are you trying to test Daddy?"

I gave him a cheeky grin around his thumb and shook my head. It was totally what I was doing, and he knew it.

Warm breath touched my face as his chest heaved, coming close enough for our noses to nearly touch. Amusement and desire glimmered in his eyes. Or I hoped that's what I could see when he carefully tugged his thumb from between my lips, making a popping sound as it left my mouth. When he put the same thumb between his lips and sucked my saliva off his thumb, the moan I released came out strangled.

A flash of molten heat rushed through my body, and I panted with how turned on I was from that single act. "Daddy," I whispered needily.

The thumb came out and the same hand cupped my cheek, bringing me closer as he bent further to touch his damp lips to mine. Barely there, they felt more like air brushing over my lips. He moved and nibbled on the corner of my lip. Needy noises slipped from me as he teased me with his mouth.

His hand slipped around my neck and held on, keeping me in the same position as I was, easily offering him control.

When his lips fully pressed against mine, my dick was achingly hard and my underwear was sticky with my need. "Beautiful boy," he murmured as his lips glided over mine in soft, unhurried caresses.

Our gazes locked as he eased back, and I could see my need reflected at me. "We need to stop if we want to enjoy the night."

A giggle burst out of me. "Daddy, I was enjoying my night," I exclaimed cheekily.

The door behind us opened and Weston stepped away and shielded me from whoever had come into the room. "Oh good, you're ready. We're about to start," I heard Zeke say.

I glanced down at my body and kept my thoughts to myself on that assumption while I worked to think of something to get my dick to behave.

Chapter Eleven

Weston

It was hard to concentrate on what I was supposed to be doing when it was much more fun to watch Matty slip into himself. As he got comfortable and started having fun, his Little side appeared while he played with the spray paints. His earlier worry about referring to me as 'Daddy' in front of others no longer seemed to be an issue.

"Daddy look what I did!" he called to me. His grin was pure joy as he swung to me, green paint on one side of his face and down the front of his T-shirt.

The guy to his left gave us what appeared to be a disapproving look, which I ignored as I promptly went to admire what Matty had done. Initially, his art work was more practiced but now it had a definite childish appearance. The bold splashes of color clashed horribly.

I ran a hand down his back and patted his bottom, matching his grin as I admired his handy work. "It's beautiful, Pumpkin. It looks like a color bomb exploded on your canvas. Daddy will need to get it framed for you."

He wrinkled his nose as he stared at the canvas, his head tilting one way then the other. "Can we find a special place to hang it?" A shyness that I wasn't used to seeing from him came with a fluttering of long blond eyelashes. "In Daddy's home..."

His hesitation brought my gaze directly to his. "Of course. You can pick a place if you like."

His reaction to this was immediate. He quivered like an excited dog, his whole body moving at once. "Tomorrow? Can we do it tomorrow, Daddy?" he squealed. His smile revealed pearly white teeth that could have sold toothpaste in a commercial.

"I'm not sure I can find a framer by tomorrow, Pumpkin." His smile disappeared and made me feel like a complete heel at how crestfallen he looked. His shoulders drooped and his lips slid into a sulky pout. "What about we pick a spot tomorrow, then go find a framer and you can see what frame you want?"

His happiness came back in a hug that got paint rubbed over the front of my T-shirt when he buried his face right into my chest and nuzzled. "Thank you, Daddy."

I ran a hand through the curls at the front of his forehead and pushed them back, leaning down to kiss his forehead. "All Daddy wants is to make my sweet boy happy," I murmured against his warm skin, meaning every word.

Was it too soon for such declarations?

Possibly.

Matty wasn't running for the hills, so that had to mean something?

~/~/~/~

I banged my head against the door I'd just shut and breathed deep, working on reminding myself that getting to know someone outside the bedroom was important. Matty appeared to be making it his mission in life to make me forget my rules. When I'd dropped him home, nudging him inside after several sweet kisses, the temptation to follow him in had been gut wrenching.

Gods how he'd looked, all soft, warm, and snuggly in my arms. All I'd wanted to do was go in and wash off all the paint and...

Reaching for the switch by the door, I flooded the room with light, cursing at how much my cock ached at thoughts of what would have come next. Light bounced off the large glass expanse that looked out over Lake Michigan. The Ferris wheel was in full view, the colorful lights a focal point at night. Roaming to the window, I adjusted my hard cock, attempting to make it more comfortable, a state that was impossible when spending time with Matty. Especially when he let go and decided to fully be himself. It was heady. Intoxicating like no liquor had ever been. I was jonesing for my next hit and I'd only left him half-an-hour ago.

I stood staring out, only seeing Matty's cute expression. He filled my thoughts and made it hard to keep things at a pace that didn't push him too fast. This last week made me greedy for more time with him. The intensity of how I felt towards him was clearer tonight as I tried to recall if ever being with a partner who'd so freely been themselves in public with me had made me feel so... whole. There was something so freeing about Matty when he was just being himself. No barriers, just him reveling in the joy of life fully. Had years of being restricted made me more cautious with previous partners? I didn't want to think it had, but I suspected it may be part of the reason none of those relationships had lasted. Time with Matty gave me a unique perspective and I liked how it made me feel, deep to my core.

When I looked at Matty, I could see a future, something I'd never considered with previous boys, if I was being truly honest. There was always something that held me back. Was it just timing? Serendipity? Working for Warner and Austin? Returning to Chicago? Matty being best friends with Austin's partner? All of it?

I ran a hand through my hair, my fingers catching in some clumped strands. That made me peer at the window to see a flash of green paint in my hair. Chuckling, I spun around and headed to the bedroom.

Stopping in the hallway, I glanced down the corridor to the other closed doors. The shower I wanted was forgotten as I recalled Matty would come for a visit the next day, to pick a space for his artwork. His continued enthusiasm had led me to seek out Zeke, who had advised we could go in and collect the pieces we'd made mid-morning on Saturday.

Plans for the next day were a little more fluid as I'd not actually planned anything other than collecting Matty for brunch. Thoughts of what we could do the next day got my feet moving on past my bedroom, down to the room I'd once used as a playroom. Opening the door, I flicked on the light and sighed at the emptiness. The hard wood floor gleamed in the overhead spotlights and cast shadows on the bare, pale lemon walls.

I walked into the middle of the large empty room, envisioning all the things that Matty might like. His playroom in Gaines' home was an eclectic mix of toys that reflected both their likes. Would he like a Little's bed I could tuck him into for naptime? A rocking chair to snuggle with me for story time?

They were all things I wanted, but would Matty want them?

Ask him!

Turning, I headed out of the room, other ideas forming as I slipped a hand into my jean pocket to retrieve my cell phone. Not overthinking it, I dialed Austin after checking the time. At ten thirty, I hoped it wasn't too late to call.

"You better have a good reason for ringing me," Austin said, his tone more amused than pissed. "You only left Matty here a short while ago."

"Is Gaines within earshot?" I answered, ignoring his comments.

"Yes."

I hesitated, chewing on my lower lip, undecided if what I was about to do was a good idea. Could asking Gaines about what Matty liked come across as snooping?

"If you've called to heavy-breath down the phone, I can tell you I ain't interested."

Laughing at him, I shook my head. "Dick. Can you put me on speakerphone so I can talk to Gaines?" His answer was a rustle against the speaker. "Gaines?"

"I'm here," a sleepy voice said.

"Listen, I'm sorry to interrupt your evening. I was just wondering if you could give me some clues about what Matty would like in a playroom."

There was an excited squeal, much the same as Matty did when he was happy about something. "Are you going to give him his own playroom? He's always wanted one of his own."

I grinned to myself, then it dimmed at the significance of Matty never having had his own space. "Do you think I should let him pick out what he wants, then?" I asked, my heart tripping over itself at how I wanted to be the one to give Matty something he'd never had before.

"Erm... yes... no... oh, this is so hard." He sighed loudly and I could hear Austin say something, just not loud enough for me to make out what it was.

I stayed silent, waiting for them to finish. Moments later, Gaines spoke up. "Matty likes to be independent most of the time. The Daddies he's had, well, they've never really taken care of all his needs. Most of the time it was about what they wanted." Another sigh came, only this time it was softer, more depressing. "Matty isn't as self-assured as he comes across. I think that's why he attracts losers..."

I laughed at how abruptly Gaines stopped speaking, clearly realizing what he'd just said when choked laughter came from Austin. "Oh crap, I'm sorry, that sounded awful. I didn't mean you, I swear."

"It's fine." I assured him. "I'm confident enough to know I don't fit in that category."

"Cocky much," Austin said, through his laughter.

"You'd never have let me within an inch of Matty if you thought I was a douchebag," I pointed out, knowing my friend well enough to figure he'd never have asked me to check out Peter and help Matty.

"True dat." A moment of silence followed. "Can I make a suggestion?"

"I'll take whatever you got."

"When Matty came in tonight, he looked so damn happy. Just be you. Do you."

Frowning into the empty room, I considered what Austin was saying. "Is it that simple?"

"Yes," said two voices at once.

Chapter Twelve

Matty

Inhaling Weston's aftershave--which filled the interior of the car—I hoped it would settle the nerves that had worked their way through my entire body. There was something different about Weston this morning, only I wasn't sure what it was that set off the jumping beans in my belly. We'd collected our artwork and Weston had carefully placed them on the back seat. We were now headed to his apartment.

Was he nervous about me seeing his home? *Possibly.* Only I wasn't totally sure it was just that.

He chatted almost nervously. "When I searched the internet, I found several framers, all close to my apartment. One said they were happy to do whatever we wanted. I thought we could drop off the artwork, then go for a stroll."

A stroll? Wasn't he going to let me pick a spot for the artwork on his wall like he promised first?

One quick twist in my seat and I got a better look at the side of Weston's face, searching his expression. Had I done something that made him change his mind? Gaines was always saying I needed to be more forthright when things felt off to me and go with my instincts. He was right. I'd know long before Peter had cheated things weren't right between us. I'd not listened.

Look how that turned out!

Problem was, emotions between me and Weston were... stronger. They had more of a depth of connection in such a short period and I felt on shaky ground. Second guessing myself, I considered if my behavior the night before gave him call to pull away.

If I said something now, would I end up tumbling off a cliff edge I couldn't see and end up broken hearted?

I sighed, grinding my teeth together at my indecision when I could recall how amazing the evening had been and how freeing it was to be Little with no restrictions. A first for me.

"Why the big sigh? Is something troubling you, Pumpkin?" Weston's eyes left the traffic for a second, and I could see the concern crinkling the corners of his eyes. Whereas the tone of voice gave nothing away.

"Did I do something wrong?" I blurted out, blushing furiously.

The car slowed dramatically, and a horn honked loudly as a truck shot past us so fast Weston's car shuddered. "Dick," he muttered crossly.

Then he glanced at me, and it threw me into a tailspin by the horror etched into his face. I kept silent, not wanting to cause any more issues when he said nothing, continuing to navigate through traffic white knuckled.

When he came to a barrier leading into an underground car park, I remained silent and watchful. He pulled into a numbered spot and turned the engine off, exhaling loudly.

Looking forward was easier than getting a dose of disappointment. When warm fingers touched the back of my tightly clasped hands, I jolted in the seat, lowering my gaze to the fingers stroking over the back of my hand.

I released a shuddery breath and twisted my neck to look sideways. *He couldn't be mad at me if he was being gentle, could he?*

Before I could start playing a guessing game that I knew would lead me on a merry dance, I bravely met Weston's gaze when he spoke.

"Why do you think you've done something wrong?" The quietness of his voice left me straining to hear him.

A temptation to look away from the blue penetrating stare, which revealed a mix of emotions, left me squirming in my seat. He was hard to read, no matter how I tried to gauge what was going on in his head. "You're nervous. You're never normally, so it makes me think I made you like that. That you're gonna dump me 'cause I upset you."

My stomach hurt when he released my hands and shifted in his seat. He fiddled with something I couldn't see, then the seat he was on pushed back. He released his seatbelt, then reached for mine. "Could you come and sit on Daddy's lap? I need a cuddle."

Confused by what was happening when I thought he was initially rejecting me, I hesitated and blinked back the tears filming my eyes, sniffing. Then I climbed out of my seat before he could change his mind, suddenly understanding why he'd moved away. Another sniff and with a knee knocking on the door panel, I came to settle on his lap facing him. Although not in the most comfortable straddling position, with my other knee on the stick shift, I didn't care to figure out another way to sit when I wanted to feel his arms around me. I leaned closer, snuggling as close to him as my position allowed and rested a cheek against his chest. His heart thudded as hard as mine under my ear, suggesting he did indeed need a cuddle.

All that had felt off since the nervous chatter started righted itself when his powerful arms encircled me and offered me the comfort I needed. His lips brushed the top of my head before he nuzzled at my hair, inhaling deep enough to move my head on his chest. "I'm nervous because I want to give you so much. I usually take my time, not rushing into anything. With you I feel differently, and it scares me. Is it all too soon?"

My head fired back and knocked into his chin hard enough to make my head ache. Only I was so focused on what he'd said, I didn't register that I could have hurt him too.

"How is it too soon?" I demanded, watching him as he rubbed his chin, then at his watery eyes.

His chuckle rumbled up his chest. "You are adorable."

I grinned, my anxiety lessening at how honest he sounded. "I am, Daddy."

The rumbling laughter increased as he shook his head. "Modest too, I see."

Cheekiness I never could hide came to the fore as I moved closer to plant a kiss on his quivering lips. "It's a cross I have to bear."

"Then I'll need to remember to share the burden with you." He winked at me right before he kissed me softly. The feel of his lips moving over mine brought a groan of approval. I could taste the lingering flavor of mint and a hint of coffee as he deepened the kiss, a hand sliding into the hair at the base of my skull, holding me as his lips danced over mine. I groaned in complaint as I shifted, wanting to get closer despite my knee pushing into the door painfully.

Dazed, I stared up at Weston when he stopped kissing me and deep furrows appeared between his brows as he looked to where my knee had gotten jammed awkwardly.

"Pumpkin, we need to stop."

"We do?" I attempted to shuffle my ass closer to him, getting a moan as it contacted with hardness.

His chuckle came with a soft, breathy curse. "Shit." He rested his forehead against mine, looking pained. "Pumpkin, we're in a parking area that has security cameras."

I fluttered my eyelashes at him. "Is that the only reason you want to stop?"

Breath ghosted my cheeks as he looked to contemplate his answer. That wasn't great for my ego and I stiffened, getting a gentle touch to my back. "When I touch you in such an intimate way, I don't want it to be in the car where I can't explore your body and find what makes you sigh with pleasure or cry out..." he came forward until his lips were right there, begging me to taste them, "or beg me to repeat what I'm doing."

His deep voice was a caress as much as what he was saying, working their magic on my overheated skin as he painted imagery in my mind. My shaky hand reached for the door handle and attempted to press on anything I could find to get it open.

Silvery brows rose and more chuckles came from the rather amused looking man. "What are you doing, Pumpkin?"

I cried in triumph as the door opened and I nearly tumbled to the floor in my haste to get out. My knee connected with Weston's solid thigh as I clambered off him and thankfully didn't land on my ass with his steadying hand.

"Getting out of the car, Daddy," I pointed out impatiently, when he didn't move. "We need to go into your apartment to do…" I fidgeted on the spot, trying to find the right words to not sound desperate when that was exactly what I was. I wanted to be naked and have his hands on me… now. Not tomorrow, not the day after, right now.

He slowly got out of the car, shutting the door before he went to the back of the car.

What is he doing?

When he had the door open and reached inside, I rolled my eyes when he stood holding our artwork.

Oh gods, he can't still want to go to the framer's first, does he? Doesn't he feel the same need to get naked?

I glanced down at the obvious bulge at the front of his slacks and I released a sigh of relief.

Why isn't he wanting to rip my clothes off?

He tucked the artwork carefully under his arm and locked the car, then offered his hand to me. "Daddy… what are we doing?"

"What does it look like, Pumpkin?"

Sweetness, his tone was full of it. Only, I wanted hotness. Back to squirming, I wrapped my fingers around his, feeling the rough ridges from his workouts. Shivers ran through me at thoughts of that roughness running over my skin.

"Like you're sticking to the plan." I tugged at the curls at the side of my head and looked up at him from under my eyelashes. "Can we do the other thing you mentioned in the car instead?" Blushing at the way the blue of his eyes deepened, I pushed on, wanting him to see I was ready for more than kisses. "We can get the pictures framed some other time," I pressed in a little closer, giving him my sweetest smile, "can't we?"

A blinding smile appeared, all teeth, while he grinned at me, making me feel like I had just won something very important. "We can... but I had plans to take you shopping for some things for the room I have, which makes for a great Littles playroom. I thought I'd show it to you so you could think about what might make it a perfect space for you when you come over."

Bubbles of excitement competed with the sexy ones at thoughts of shopping for a special room just for me. I groaned at my conflict because I wanted both things with equal measure.

"Daddyyy," I whined, unsure how to decide.

He tugged me through the car park towards an elevator, looking like the cat who had eaten every drop of cream from the store. "You're not playing fair, Daddy."

Inside the elevator, he kissed the top of my head before pushing a button for the fifteenth floor. "Why is that? I'm giving you options to choose from, isn't that a good thing? Would you like Daddy to pick for you instead?" Nothing about the question suggested he would get annoyed at either option.

This was a hard one because normally my partners in the past had never let it occur to them to consider what I wanted. It was lovely that he was offering me the choice, except I wanted both. "I want both, Daddy. Can I have both?"

A look I was coming to recognize suggested he was considering how to achieve that for me. Back to the bubbly feeling, the lift came to a stop on the floor we needed. He ushered me out first, then led me down a thickly carpeted hallway to his apartment. He slipped his free hand into his jacket and pulled out his keys, unlocked the door and then pushed it open. He stepped in first and deactivated a security system that looked as high tech as the one in Austin's building.

He carefully placed our artwork on a table that was off to the left in the wide, L-shaped room. My gaze traveled to the large glass windows that looked out over Lake Michigan and to the Chicago skyline. My attention was held by the view and it took a little longer to register the homely feeling the place offered. He'd covered the wooden floors with thick gray patterned rugs. There were what looked like comfortable couches, with big cushions sitting on them and he had positioned the furniture to make the most of the view. One lone chair sat in front of a white wall holding a flat screen TV. To the right there was a double doorway that I peeked through, which led into a dining and kitchen area. The view from those windows was no less spectacular.

It was easy to envision myself sitting at the table playing while Weston cooked for us. "You have a beautiful home." As I said it, I realized I meant every word. It was *a home*.

Although, he didn't have many knickknacks scattered around or an abundance of furniture. Every piece had a sense of purpose that added to the overall feel that I could settle right in and be right at home with no effort.

"Thank you," he murmured from behind me. His hands sat on my hips as he brought me back to rest against his body. His familiar scent and the press of his solid body against me gave me a boost of joy.

"Do you want to look at the room I've picked out?"

The softly spoken question brought my attention from the view and I slowly moved within his hold. When facing him, I tilted back my head, searching for any clues to what he wanted to do. "I'd love to see all the rooms, Daddy... especially yours."

Lips moved into a soft smile as he traced a finger over my cheekbone, then brushed back an unruly curl. It had been a few weeks since I'd decided to cut my hair and the curls were growing back in a wayward style that I could do little about if I wanted to grow them again.

He held my gaze for what felt like minutes rather than seconds before stepping back, his hand dropping to interlace his fingers with mine. "Let's start here."

I could see no point in arguing, as we were already in the living area. So I listened as he explained how many rooms were in the apartment as he took me on a tour. In the kitchen and dining space, he pointed out the balcony, which had seats and a table, all covered. "It's a great place in the summer to sit in the evening and watch the sun set."

He pointed out features that living so high up came with and my love of the place grew as he painted pictures of how he liked to spend his time in his home. There were photos of his parents. I knew his father had died the year before because Austin had mentioned it. In the picture of him and his parents, they were all laughing at whoever had taken the picture. It spoke of love and happiness.

When he led me out of the main area and down a hallway, I could see four additional doors. The first was a cinema room. If I'd thought the TV in the main room was large, this was humongous and covered an entire wall. "Holy cow! Why do you need such a big TV?"

His grin was sheepish as he guided me out and shut the door. "I love ice hockey. To get the full effect, sports can only be watched on the big screen or live."

My lips twitched at how serious he sounded and it reminded me again of how much he loved sporting activities. "Do you go to many games?"

"No, but I hope to change that now I'm home." A boyish smile charmed me and I could see myself getting caught up in his enthusiasm if I wasn't careful.

The next door was the family bathroom. It had a bath with a tap set off at an angle at one end. The tub was large enough for two people and the tap placement meant neither would get jabbed. Was that on purpose? Did he like to get in the bath with his boy?

The buzz that came this time had everything to do with the idea of having bath time with Weston. Fingers waved in front of my face and I blinked twice, noticing Weston was more inside the bathroom than he had been a moment or two ago. I bit my lower lip, giving him a shy look, though I suspected he knew exactly where my thoughts had traveled.

"What was going on in your head, Pumpkin?"

I shrugged, working to stop the blush heating my skin. "What a nice *big* bath you have."

His lips brushed against my ear as he bent down and whispered, "All the better to share with you, little Pumpkin."

Giggling at how he said it like he was a big, bad wolf, I let him lead me back into the hallway. He pointed to the next door. "That's my bedroom. We'll go there last."

Walking to the next door, he opened it and stepped aside to let me walk in front of him. I stopped inside the doorway. The empty space benefited from the sunlight and had nothing in it to obstruct the view that rivaled all the others I'd seen. Soft yellow painted walls glowed in the light pouring from the bank of windows, as did the wooden floor the sun reflected off. The built-in closet door was open, showing it was as empty as the room.

"As you can see, it's a blank canvas." Back was the nervousness I'd heard in the car.

I swung around, arms wide, the thrill running wild at what he was offering me. At what it meant. "This is for me to do with as I want?" I double checked, wanting to make sure I was hearing and reading him right. In the past, I'd made too many errors to trust myself.

He casually leaned against the door frame, watching me, his arms crossing over his chest. "Absolutely, Pumpkin. I want you to be my boy... full time. I know your home is with Gaines, but I'd like you to consider this your home too. To do that, I want to help make that possible in whatever way works for you."

Ideas of getting naked had a full on war with the need to go out and find things to make the room mine. I ran and jumped at Weston, who caught me in his arms, laughing as I peppered kisses over his face, puncturing them occasionally with, "thank you," while I rode the wave of my happiness.

"You're welcome, my Pumpkin."

Chapter Thirteen

Weston

Matty seemed to bounce from one emotion to another. He was hard to keep up with. I got he wasn't good at always asking for what he wanted when it came to important things so I considered my actions carefully. In the car, I sensed that he was ready to move ahead with the more intimate side of our relationship, right up until he got offered the room to do with as he wanted. I never considered deterring Matty from his mission to find things for the playroom instead of what I'd originally planned when we'd kissed in the car. The wonder that shone brighter than any star in the night sky, when he'd gotten the room was his to do with as he pleased, would combat any need to keep that look on his face.

When he finally wiggled down my body, causing me to swallow a groan at his pert ass doing a number on my cock, I'd let him drag me out of the room, chatting ten to the dozen. "What shops should we go to first? There are lots around this part of town. I'm sure there are. We need a big toy shop and a furniture store. But we need one that will have things I like. I can be very picky." He grinned, not seeming in the least bit concerned about his confession as I reset the alarm to exit the apartment.

He waited until we were back in the elevator before he resumed with the excited questioning. "I need to check my bank account, see how much I have to spend." His brow furrowed for a split second, then smoothed out. "I've been good of late, so I should have enough to get some nice things. Do you think they'll have furniture with fox designs on them? I've seen some on different websites."

"There's a furniture store I've used before, Room & Board, directly down East Ohio Street about six minutes' walk from here. They have many things you might like to look at." I recalled the bed that was like a small wooden house that was cute. I could see him in there with me reading him a story, but I'd go with whatever he wanted. "Fox designs, though? If you have something specific you want, it might require more of a wide search to get it." I pointed out, unsure right now he'd be patient enough with how excited he was. "And I think we need to discuss money before we get to the shop."

I directed him out of the front of the building, just offering a wave at the person staffing the main reception as we passed, making a mental note to introduce Matty to them so they'd know not to stop him from coming into the building.

His feet dragged a little as I slowed down when we hit the street. "I've got money, Daddy."

Hints of uncertainty were easy to pick up as he brought his thumb up to his lips, looking at it for a second before chewing on the nail. Seeing this could be an issue for him, I moved us out of the way of those walking up and down the street, considering if we should go back into the building to have a private conversation. Only, the way he looked with big eyes begging me to carry on made him hard to resist.

"Has money been an issue between you and past boyfriends?" I asked in a low tone, aware of those coming past us. I kept the terms I used more generic.

"Some," he mumbled past the thumb.

Carefully, I eased his thumb from between his teeth, wiping it while I crouched to meet his gaze. "Do you have a problem with me spending money on you?" I went for directness, recalling Austin and Gaines' suggestion I just be me. I wanted to give Matty everything his heart desired, but only if he wanted that, too.

A wrinkle appeared at the top of his nose as he continued to stare, his head tilting to the left, then the right, as if he was trying to gauge something. "Do you want to spend money on me?" he asked, instead of answering my question.

Resisting the chuckle that tickled the back of my throat at his obvious avoidance, I nodded. "Yes, I do. I was hoping you would give in to Daddy and go a little wild." I came in closer, grinning. "Daddy has to confess he can find it a little hard to let go when it comes to spending, so I need my Pumpkin to show me how much fun it is."

He eyed me the way a child would when they were searching for a potential pitfall, whilst clearly not seeing anything wrong with the logic of having everything they wanted. "Are you sure?"

Although he asked, there was little doubt in my mind he'd already decided when I nodded. "Yep." I gave in and brushed a kiss over his parted lips, enjoying the taste of his sweetness. "Wanna go spend Daddy's money?" The answering grin was so wide it was all teeth. "Then let's go."

~/~/~/~

Chris, the shop assistant we'd found in the store, was friendly and not too pushy, both a bonus when Matty was back to asking lots of questions and not giving anyone time to answer them. After the third attempt by Chris to answer him, I decided to intervene. "What about you and I stroll around the store and see if there is anything that catches your eye?"

Looking at the sign that pointed to a large display of children's furniture up on the next level, Matty nodded absently. "Do you think they'll have a bed up there to fit me?"

Chris, for a moment, wore a startled expression before he blushed and looked down at the ground. "Some children's beds have extendable frames. They should say on the shop tag."

"Great, thank you. We'll come back if we find something we like," I said, smiling reassuringly at Chris, who glanced up, giving me a look that made me consider he might be into the scene.

Off and running, Matty was already at the steps leading up to the section where the children's furniture was before I'd moved. I followed at a slower pace, enjoying watching him bounce around, clearly enjoying himself as he looked about.

It didn't take long for him to spot something he liked. I could tell instantly what bed had captured his attention. Becoming motionless, he stood, his mouth forming an O shape as he stared at the little treetop bed. It had a top canopy over it that looked like the branches of a tree. Hand tooled wood laced together to form leaf patterns. Interwoven were small fairy lights which were switched on, reflecting little shadows over the lemon bedding, making it appear like stars were shining down through the leaves.

A small stepladder led up to the bed and I could see that Matty had already made his mind up about wanting it before he glanced around to find me, his expression revealing hope.

"It's beautiful," I pointed out approvingly.

"It is..."

He shifted his attention to the information tag, uncertainty clouding his eyes. I moved quickly to block his view. Nothing would stop me from buying that bed and keeping him happy. "Is there anything else you see that might go with the bed? I think we need a cabinet to store the toys we're gonna buy."

That got him twirling to look around and we were off once more.

Two hours later, starving and unsure where Matty got his energy for shopping when he didn't like to exercise, we exited the shop having fitted out the bedroom with furniture. I'd paid extra to have the in store furniture delivered and set up while we continued on our shopping spree. I'd done this while Chris had taken Matty to see a set of rainbow furniture. A small table and chair set that fit his slight frame perfectly that I had to get, too.

Outside the shop, after a quick call to organize the delivery of the furniture to my apartment when Matty went to use the restroom, I summoned a Lyft to take us for lunch then it was on to a toy shop I'd visited before, Timeless Toys. It had everything a Little could want, and more.

Matty watched me, clinging to my free hand, which he was swinging between us, unusually quiet for him. "Are you hungry?"

His sneakered foot kicked at the ground. "I thought we were going toy shopping?"

"Food first, then toys." It was hard not to laugh when he sighed and let his whole body slump.

"Can't we get food afterwards? Please, Daddy?" Out came the big guns, eyelids fluttering, while he tugged at a curl.

He was a temptation, for sure. "Food, then toys," I said firmly, in my Daddy voice, when he looked to argue with me, and his smile dimmed. "We'll go to Portillo's for hotdogs, they have crinkle fries too."

Instantly, his smile brightened. "They do?"

A quick grin and I checked the app for where the car was. Barely a hundred yards away, I checked the street. It pulled up seconds later, and I ushered Matty into the back seat. The traffic was murder mid-afternoon, so it took a little longer to get lunch.

By the time we'd eaten, it was late afternoon and Matty was on an ice cream high. The boy had a bottomless stomach when it came to sweet things. Problem was, his enthusiasm was contagious and I was possibly as giddy as him when we reached the toy shop.

Within ten minutes of being inside the shop, Matty had slipped into his Little space. The shopping cart he'd grabbed danced and weaved as he went down the aisles, his ass swaying in time to whatever tune he was humming to himself. He'd pause now and then, checking to make sure I was right with him.

Periodically he'd stop and look a little closer at the toys, his hands going behind his back almost like it scared him to touch.

The cart remained empty and I wondered if I needed to intervene when he exclaimed, "Ohhhh look, I knew they'd be here somewhere, foxes! All the foxes, Daddy, see!" In the next second he'd released the cart and darted to a display he'd found of his favored animal.

A couple with a toddler of maybe three years old glanced at Matty disapprovingly, only he was so lost in himself he didn't appear to notice. They rushed away, the sound of tutting loud enough for me to hear when I gave them a hard stare.

Matty turned and waved a hand, summoning me. "Come see," he demanded impatiently.

Amping up my smile when he got a small wrinkle between his brows, I walked towards him. "What have you found?"

Chapter Fourteen

Matty

Exhausted, I struggled to keep my eyes open as I waited for Weston to take the remaining shopping bags from the trunk of the car. Today had been one of the best days of my life, where I was the sole focus of someone who wanted me to be happy. Yes, I'd had some wonderful times with Gaines, but this was different because it was with Weston. He's given me all of his attention throughout the full day. I'd seldom, if ever, experienced that.

The door behind me swished open and a man appeared dressed in what looked like a uniform of pressed navy slacks, white shirt, and navy jacket, and came to a stop in front of me. He glanced from me to Weston and back. "Can I help you, Sir?"

Weston used his elbow to shut the trunk and came towards us, offering the man a polite smile. "It's fine William. This is Matty, my partner."

"Are you sure you don't need a hand, sir?" he asked, not looking back at me but showing interest in the large number of shopping bags Weston held with the toy shop name over them.

"No, we can manage. Although while I have you, could you ensure Matty is added to the list of approved people who can come into the building, please?"

"Of course, sir."

He was so polite I expected he'd walk like he had a pole up his backside when he swung around, once again not looking in my direction as he entered the building. We followed behind him, Weston not seeming to notice how stiff William was, so I suspected it was his normal way of behaving.

At the large reception desk Weston stopped and, while juggling the bags, took the electronic key card William offered him as they chatted about mundane stuff.

A few minutes later, in the elevator, I stared at the key card Weston offered me. "This will give you entry into the building if no one is around on the reception to let you in. The desk is staffed day and night, but there can be periods of time when they are busy, so the main doors get locked and require a key card to get into the building."

The simple explanation didn't denote the weight of what he was offering me. Having been in Little space, sometimes big stuff was harder to wrap my head around and I stared at the card. Why I felt it was a big deal after he'd spent thousands of dollars on creating a space for my benefit, possibly had something to do with finding Peter cheating with Richard when he'd given me a key to his place and I'd gone in blindly.

His brows drew together as his eyes narrowed on me. "What's up, Pumpkin?"

I shrugged, struggling to voice how overwhelmed I was feeling. Would he understand my worries?

The door opened and instead of finding an answer, I stepped out, feeling the weight of Weston's stare very much as he followed.

Inside the apartment, with a little more juggling to get the door open and turn a switch that illuminated two lamps sat either end of the large sofa, giving a warm glow to the room, I noticed the key card remained clutched in his fingers. Door shut and three steps further into the apartment, he dropped the bags, moving the card to slip into the pocket of his slacks.

I sighed dejectedly, feeling like I'd potentially ruined the day.

"Pumpkin, what do you need from Daddy?"

The straightforwardness of the question helped ease the tension crawling inside me as fast as ants scurrying to escape being trampled on. "Can I sit on Daddy's lap to cuddle? I'm tired."

He took the bags I was continuing to clutch and placed them next to the pile he'd deposited on the rug, appearing unconcerned they were cluttering the middle of the floor. In one motion he scooped me up, getting a little hiccupped breath to catch in my throat at the show of strength. He cradled me to his chest, his jacket cool against my cheek from the crispness of the air outside. He walked to the couch and sat facing the bank of windows showing a darkening sky and tucked me against him.

Silence descended between us in the room's quiet. He brushed his lips over my hair and my eyelids drifted shut. I let the sleep tug me under, needing just this—to be held.

~/~/~/~

Unsure what startled me awake, I blinked the room into focus, noting at once how dark it was outside and that I remained cuddled against Weston. Although he was relaxed, I suspected he wasn't asleep by the way his arms held me tight against him.

As I lay there, I pondered what I should do or say about what had happened earlier. Would he still want me to have the key card after my reaction, or lack thereof?

"Are you hungry?" What alerted him to my wakefulness, I wasn't sure, as I was positive I'd remained still. He delivered the softly spoken question in a tone that suggested he didn't want to disturb the peace or possibly spook me. Which, given the circumstances, I got with my behavior earlier.

The empty feeling in the pit of my stomach got me nodding, then tilting back my head to look up at him, wanting to see his expression. "I'm sorry."

"What do you have to be sorry for, Pumpkin?" He kissed me, a smile tugging at his mouth, reassuring me more than his words.

Little sparks fluttered in my belly. "I didn't... take... the key card," I stuttered.

"Are you able to tell me why?" His gaze held mine, offering encouragement.

"It felt big to me. After coming out of little space, sometimes I struggle to deal with the big stuff."

His nod was slow and considered, as if he sensed it wasn't the whole truth and he'd be right. "How do you feel now? Do you want to talk about it?"

I watched him carefully, looking for any signs of annoyance as I contemplated what to say. "I got spooked." Breathing became a little easier as he smiled encouragingly at me. "Recalling how bad it turned out having access to putrid Peter's place. Not that I'm saying you're anything like him." I scrubbed my hands over my face, working on collecting my thoughts while Weston remained silent.

It's Weston, he'll understand!

Hands clenching together in my lap, I bravely met his gaze once more. "I felt vulnerable after having such a wonderful day. Being Little normally requires some consideration to get me in the right head-space... with you, it happens with no effort." I gave him an imploring look. "Have you ever been terrified, the kind that makes you feel you might be sick and never stop?"

"Yes." Everything about his expression denoted the seriousness of that one word.

"That's how I feel about losing you. You said it earlier. It's too soon, but my heart is one hundred percent invested and if it doesn't work out... it will break me like Peter never could." As I uttered the words, I knew it was at the core of my fear. Peter hurt me, bruised my ego. Weston held the power to crush me. I sucked in a shuddery breath, then released it and took a leap of faith. "I want the key card. Please, Daddy, I do."

"Are you sure that's what you want, and it's not about pleasing me? I want you here, just to be clear and those scary feelings aren't one sided as I mentioned earlier. Also, I'm going to clarify, I've never once cheated on a partner. If we were having problems, then we'd talk them out, because losing you is not on any agenda, now or in the future."

The kiss he gave me was just the hint of flesh touching flesh, yet it was so much more with how he held my gaze. "So, are you sure?"

"Yes. I slept on it." I grinned cheekily at him, hoping to break the tension I'd caused with my confession. "On you. I want it, please."

Still wearing his jacket, he moved me, and his hand wiggled under my hip before the key card appeared in front of my face. I snatched the warm plastic and felt a wave of dizziness when he beamed at me when I gleefully hugged it to my chest.

"So, are you hungry? I've got the making for a peanut butter and jelly sandwich, if you're interested."

"Is it grape jelly? I love grape. And the crunchy peanut butter?" I bounced at his nod before he shifted his weight, not letting go of me as he came up to standing, giving me a sudden boost of warm fuzzies.

In the kitchen, he sat me on a high stool next to the island in the center of the room, leaving to go to the refrigerator. Feeling the warmth of the room, I tucked the card into my pocket before slipping off my coat.

"Let me take that for you." Weston laid down the jars he held to take the coat from me. Moving confidently around the room, he slipped my coat onto the back of a chair, then slipped off his own. The button-down beneath his jacket had become a mass of wrinkles and my fingers itched to flatten them.

"What juice do you want, orange, apple or cranberry?"

Distracted by the question, I tapped my lip. "Apple, please."

Once I had my juice, I hummed in satisfaction when he moved my finger to give me a brief kiss before continuing to make me a sandwich.

It was fun to watch him as he made me a plate of food and added chips on the side with slices of apple, putting it in front of me with a flourish. He placed another sandwich on a plate, pushing it over to the space next to me, not taking the same care he'd done with mine.

When he took the stool and twisted to face me, I waited. In the restaurant we'd eaten at, he'd cut up my food and placed everything within easy reach for me. I suspected now we were alone he'd want to help. I grinned at him when he offered me the sandwich to nibble on while he took a large bite out of his own. He fed himself and me and in between bites I sipped at the glass of juice, staring at him.

"When did you figure out you might prefer being a daddy?" I asked, after swallowing the last mouthful of apple.

He brushed off the crumbs on his fingers, finished his drink, then placed an elbow on the counter in front of him. Resting his cheek in his hand, tiny grooves developed around his eyes. "Not rightly sure, in and around my late twenties. I dated a guy who was several years older than me, and though I didn't initially notice, he encouraged me to take charge. Small things at first, like where we should go on a date. Ordering food for him. Then it progressed to taking the initiative on most things, which he loved. I was away a lot, and I noticed he wasn't coping with life stuff during the time apart. Things I'd expect would be easy weren't. So by mutual agreement, the relationship ended. It was a couple of years later, I understood why."

"He was a boy at heart who wanted a full time Daddy?" I guessed separation could be hard on any relationship, but for someone who liked the dynamic of a daddy/boy relationship, it could be more so.

"Yes. I met him and his new boyfriend out in a club I enjoyed going to that catered to the kink lifestyle. All three of us talked a little about the past and after they'd left, I considered what he'd said about me being nurturing and how that worked for men who were looking for a Daddy."

He reached out and stroked his fingers over the back of my hand, which sat next to my empty glass. Warmth spread through me at the simple touch. Getting to know him, I figured he contemplated talking about ex partners might be hard on me. It wasn't though, because we weren't talking about my exes. "So, that was the beginning?"

"It took a few more years before I found a guy that was interested in forming that type of relationship. Only work got in the way again, as he didn't enjoy being left with the uncertainty of my job. Much like Warner, and even Austin, it's hard being gay and kinky when in the forces. Too many restrictions." He shrugged and that slow smile that lit him up from the inside out appeared. "I believe the universe just decided I needed to wait for the right boy to come along."

I hopped off the stool and hugged my arms around his waist, causing him to sit up straight and reach to hold on to me or fall off the seat. "I'm glad the universe knew what they were doing," I whispered, squeezing him hard.

"Me too... now do you think you're ready to put away the new toys and check out the room?"

Head firing back to look up, I searched his expression, my pulse tripping over itself. "Put away the toys? There's no furniture in my room," I pointed out, then wriggled at the way he grinned at me.

"I paid for delivery and set-up. William let them in so they could..."

I didn't hear the rest as I was already racing to the room Weston had given me. At the door, I stopped dead. The moonlight and reflection of lights from the other buildings outside cast the room in shadows but still gave me enough light to make out where the bed and cabinets we'd bought were positioned. My hand went to my mouth and I sucked in a sob.

The light turned on and Weston was there, his powerful arms wrapping around me as I cried at how much better the bed looked sitting in the room. "Look at my bed," I mumbled around the next sob.

Weston's chin pressed to the top of my head, my back firmly against his chest as he cocooned me in his arms. I could feel the steady beat of his heart as he kept me close and let me ride my emotional outburst. "It's all so pretty."

"Not as pretty as you, but yes, it looks good." He kissed my hair, and I could feel the smile on his lips. "You know what will make it better? All your new toys. Shall we get you something to blow your nose? Then you can sort your toys while I put the new bed linen on so you can try out your tree bed."

The need to do all of that at once got me spinning in Weston's arms. "Okay, but can I put the bed lights on first?" I titled my head, giving him a shy smile, "Please?"

Chapter Fifteen

Weston

It had taken herculean restraint to not give in and play with Matty all night long; the nap had regenerated him, along with the sandwich. We'd discussed him spending the night, only I was now envisioning myself sleeping in the tree bed with him after I'd read him yet another story. The mattress was as soft as a cloud—as promised by the manufacturer—it just wasn't made for someone as tall and wide as me, especially when Matty insisted he lie on top of me for story time.

"That's the last one, Pumpkin." I interjected enough authority to let him know I was serious, only the begging eyes were back in full force.

"Daddy... just one more, pleaseeeee? I'm so comfy." The softness of his features as he rested his chin on the hands he'd folded on my chest an hour ago was—I decided—going to be my undoing. The curls were in disarray and his lower lip was poking out in an adorable pout.

"Pumpkin, Daddy is getting a crick in his neck. It's late and we need to have a shower before getting ready for bed."

The battle light that sparked in his eyes at my denial changed to something else at the mention of the shower. He wriggled against me. "Together?"

"Sleeping? Or showering?"

Back to tilting his head, the curls tumbled over his forehead and my whole being lit up at the adorableness that was Matty. "Both."

"Yes, both," I supplied for clarity, which got a knee to the balls for my effort. I groaned at the dull ache while Matty used me to wedge himself up and off the side of the bed, ignoring the steps and jumping down.

I rubbed at my crotch as I carefully moved to avoid banging my head on the overhead canopy, giving him a stern stare.

It got lost on him when he was already heading for the door, calling out, "Daddy, how big is your shower?"

Following at a slower pace, I switched off the fairy lights and listened with half an ear to Matty as he explored my bedroom. We'd not gotten to check it out earlier, after we'd carried all the toys and books into his room. Pleasing him was easy when it came with sweet smiles and eyes glowing with happiness. He was alluring most of the time, but when he was bouncing with joy, he made me forget everything...

including my desk, where I'd left all the information I'd printed out about Peter.

Shit!

Shit!

Quickening my steps, I moved soundlessly into the bedroom and found Matty stood staring down at my desk, motionless.

"What's all this?" he asked in a high-pitched tone that hurt my ears.

I moved to stand next to him. The tension rolling off him was obvious after how relaxed he'd been in the other room. "My investigation of Peter's life."

He glanced from the desk to me. "There's pictures of me, too."

"You were part of Peter's life. When I research a person, I explore all past relationships," I explained, sliding a hand down his arm, needing to touch him as much for me as him. How we were going to spend the rest of the evening no longer felt assured.

"So you dig into my life, too?"

There was something about the way he asked that suggested he had something to hide, and the hairs on the base of my neck rose. "No, not in the way you're thinking about. I only explore how the two lives intersect. What came before or after isn't something I'm interested in."

It was instinctual to reach for him when he sagged and appeared to lose the ability to stand on his own legs. "What are you worried about?" I asked hesitantly, unsure I was going to like what he had to say.

For a moment, I thought I'd pushed in the wrong direction, and he wasn't going to answer me. "I'm a loser... I've dated some..."

Relief came, then swiftly on its heels, fury at what he meant. I kissed him, holding him close enough that I could feel his heart pounding against my chest. I kissed him with all the emotions he created deep inside. Ones that wanted to go out and hunt every asshole that had made him doubt how special he was. "You're no loser, Pumpkin. You're a special man who got taken advantage of."

The next kiss was softer as I rocked him in my arms, needing to rid him of any negative thoughts he had about himself.

When I eased back, he'd become flushed and looked more than a little dazed. Wanting to keep him that way, I carefully undressed him, kissing him in between each layer of clothing I dropped to the floor until he was naked and flushed with arousal.

His skin was soft as a rose petal as I ran my fingers down the center of his hairless chest, over waxed skin to the base of his protruding cock. Hard, pink and with a slick head, it bobbed as I lowered to my knees, focusing my attention there.

Hands hanging at his sides formed into balls as I ran a finger up the length of the silky hardness, reaching the tip. The sounds of heavy breathing came with the increased scent of arousal. It hung in the air as I slowly rotated the tip of my finger over the slickness, gathering it. I raised my gaze, holding Matty's as I brought the finger to my lips and opened to suck it in. The salty taste burst over my tongue, a combination of sweet with bitter.

He groaned as I did when I swallowed and wet my finger, removing it to run it over the mushroom head. His body shuddered at the gentle caresses, but he never pushed into my touch. Just held still and waited for me to decide.

"Daddy's boy tastes so good," I murmured before sucking the finger back into my mouth, getting another taste of him that got my dick straining against my rumpled slacks. When I removed my finger this time, I used it to stroke over the soft ball sack. I traced a wet trail down and under his balls to his taint. He widened his stance, groaning when my finger pressed behind his balls.

I watched his eyelids flutter and mouth drop open as I rubbed against the skin. Giving him no time to figure what was coming next, wanting him to lose himself purely in pleasure, I came forward and swallowed his slim cock down to the back of my throat in one move.

His cry was low and strangled. Encouraged, I swallowed to clasp the head of his pulsing cock in my throat. Already anticipating what might come next, I was prepared for his juddering hip thrust and opened my throat. My gag reflex got a workout as small hands tugged on my hair as the cock in my mouth thickened as I sucked deep.

"Ohhhhhh, that... jeez!"

I eased back and circled the crown of his cock with my tongue, murmuring against his flesh, "Come for Daddy. Let me taste you."

"Daddyyyy," he moaned and thrust repeatedly into my willing mouth with no restraint.

It didn't take but three thrusts for the first splash of cum to hit the back of my tonsils. Unable to get a full taste, I shifted back a fraction so I could feel the cum hit my tongue. My groan matched his as I gulped greedily. Wanting more, I used my tongue to prolong his release, teasing around the head before licking at the slit to get every drop.

The fingers digging in my hair went lax several moments later and Matty collapsed over me, all but resting his bent body on my head and shoulders. His chest was rising and falling fast and his breath hit the back of my neck.

"I'm wobbly," he rasped.

With some careful maneuvering, I got him to a position where I could hold him and get up off the floor with the help of my desk. The ache between my legs was unimportant, with the need to take care of the sleepy boy taking precedent. I part carried, part walked him into the bathroom and placed a towel on the toilet seat to sit him on.

One look at his dopey grin and I changed my plan of giving him a shower.

He sat quietly as I filled the sink with warm, soapy water. His blinking was so slow he appeared to be moving in slow motion. I washed and dried all the important bits as he continued to grin sleepily at me, making no effort to help. As the clothes we'd bought weren't washed, I left him naked, lifting him effortlessly off the toilet to carry the sweet smelling boy back to my bed.

One tug of the covers and I laid him on the brushed cotton sheets. He snuggled right into the mattress, a happy sigh following as I pulled the covers over his body.

I stood staring at him. At the beautiful picture this man made in my bed. His face flushed, his eyelids barely open, looking totally replete.

"Naked... Daddy," he mumbled before his eyes shut. A second later they opened, before closing and his breathing evened out.

How long I remained standing just staring at him, counting every blessing at finding this man, I couldn't say. When I stripped and went to shower, all I could think about was him in my bed. How the thoughts of him waking and leaving left me wanting the world to stop turning so I could have this moment. Live in this moment... *forever.*

Now I'd tasted a little of what life could be like with him in it, I wanted it. I wanted it all.

My head resting on the wet glass, I shut my eyes, feeling the heat of the water soak into my tense muscles. What was I going to do about that? I'd no clue, and that scared me more than anything. He wasn't the only one who could get their heart crushed whether he realized it, or not.

I blew out a shaky breath and opened my eyes to reach for the soap. "One step at a time. It's the only way. One. Step. At. A. Time."

Chapter Sixteen

Matty

Was it too much to ask for my good fortune to last? It seemed it was as I watched Peter slink into the vacant seat next to me for the last meeting of the day. When I'd woken up, naked and wrapped in Weston's arms, for the second morning, life had felt perfect. He'd given me a shower and a mind-blowing hand job that had set me up with a pep in my step for a Monday morning. The weekend had been... wonderful.

Sunday, I'd discovered sleeping naked had many benefits when it came to spreading out on top of Weston who, though solid, was very comfy to lie on. He cooked and fed me breakfast in bed. After that, we lazed about with his laptop. Ignoring everything laid on the desk tucked in the corner of his bedroom by silent agreement, we did some internet searches for prints of foxes for my bedroom. Later, we visited the framer's after I picked a spot where I wanted to hang my picture. Who knew picking a frame could be so hard? Finally, we'd gone for a very late lunch at Shaw's Crab House, a place that turned out to have the best lobster tacos. Weston's proclamation, as far as I could tell, had been correct. They'd been delicious, and I'd got a box to take home for Gaines and Austin when we'd decided I'd spend Sunday night with Weston too. He had taken me home to grab fresh clothes for Monday and a few of my little clothes to put in the closet.

Sitting next to Peter, his cologne stinking up the room, Weston threatening Peter to stay away on Friday seemed such a long time ago. My thinking he'd listen, I blamed on the endorphins that came from being with Weston. I didn't look at Peter as I fiddled with my iPad to open up the program with the design plan we were here to discuss with the clients. The large screen was positioned at the end of the boardroom table so everyone could see it. The zoom meeting was being broadcast from several parts of the States so it was the last meeting of the day to fit as many time zones as possible.

"Stop acting like I'm invisible," Peter hissed next to my ear and close enough I could tell he'd eaten garlic recently.

Not looking in his direction, I tapped at my iPad, pretending to be interested in what was on the screen. It was easier than going with my urge to poke a tongue at him.

"You think I'm scared of the guy who turned up Friday issuing threats? You're very much mistaken. He's just a wannabe daddy who's lucky I didn't smack him in the mouth." He was keeping his tone of voice down, but the anger was impossible to miss as he continued to angrily hiss directly into my ear.

The day had been good, and I'd almost made myself believe that life was back to normal. It seemed the man next to me wanted to remind me I could and had made epic errors of misjudgment, whether or not I wanted him to. A place I'd normally be content to sit and work in felt like an old shoe that dug into the soft bits of my foot from overuse.

Anger at the injustice of it all bubbled as I swung my head towards Peter and gave him a withering look. "Listen, why don't you just get over yourself? I wasn't the one who cheated. I did nothing wrong, yet you feel the need to harass me and act like an A hole. Why is that? Because aren't you the one flaunting your engagement to Richard in my face every chance you get?"

A sudden silence fell in the room, and I swallowed a groan at having allowed Peter to bait me. At best, he'd made me look foolish, and at worst, like I was the one being a dick when we were in a senior meeting, supposed to be acting professional.

The cough that came from the top of the table made me wince inwardly. "If we've quite finished having personal discussions, can we get on with the business at hand?" This came from Shaw, the managing director. He wasn't into pleasantries, but he was a fair boss. The look he cast at me suggested he wasn't happy with me.

The warmth that spread up my cheeks burned when Peter gave me a smug look as he nodded at Shaw. "Of course, I'm sorry for Matty's outburst."

Seething at him apologizing for me like I was to blame, I bit the inside of my cheek hard, to refrain from saying more.

The meeting started and it was hard to miss the looks I was getting as I did my best to concentrate and answer questions about the design I'd created. By the time the meeting ended, I could feel sweat patches under my armpits. I quickly collected my things and exited the room before Peter could trap me into saying anything more.

In my office, I slumped into the chair behind my desk, dropping all I held to bury my head in my hands.

"You should learn that I don't take too kindly to being made to look a fool," Peter stated in a harsh, nasal tone as the door to the office shut hard enough to make a point.

I sat up and glared at him, although my guts twisted tightly at the ugly expression he wore. Objectively, he was a handsome man and well dressed, in a polished kind of way that gave him a glossy veneer. That veneer hid what was underneath—a shallow man who was only interested in himself. Something I'd been too blind to see when we'd been together. "I want you to leave, now. I have nothing to say to you."

"Is that so? Well I have plenty to say. What do you think you were playing at dumping me! My life was perfect until you decided you knew better. Now I've had to get engaged and look at how that is turning out. He's spending my money like it grows on trees. This is all your damn fault," he snarled, spit flying from his mouth.

"Your life, your decisions. You made them, you choose to cheat. Did you think I would sit back meekly and let you use me like that once I knew what you were doing? I'm worth more than that. It's not my fault you've got yourself into a situation you aren't happy with." It felt good to say it. To understand some of why he'd been behaving like such an A hole.

Problem was, I'd never thought Peter to be a violent man, but the way he was staring at me suggested being in a room with the door shut was not a wise move.

Glancing at my desk, I reached for my cell phone. I took a second to find Weston's number and hit dial.

"What are you doing?" Peter sneered, stepping closer to my desk threateningly.

"Calling my Daddy," I said, adding as much bravery as I could muster while my innards were shaking so bad it made me feel like I was rocking in my seat. Weston had worked today, I just couldn't remember if he'd told me a time he'd be finished. Our plan was to meet the following night. Would he be mad at me for calling him? No, he told me to call him if Peter was horrible to me.

All these thoughts rushed through my head as I watched Peter hesitate, then lurch over my desk towards me, his hand reaching for my cell phone.

I pushed my chair back just as I heard Weston's voice asking, "This is a delightful surprise, Pumpkin. How's my sweet boy?"

"Daddy, help me," I shouted in Peter's face. "Peter's in my office being horrible."

The cell phone flew out of my hand in fright as Peter mounted my desk to get to the cell phone.

I could hear Weston's voice calling from somewhere on the floor where my cell landed, only I was too busy working to avoid the man sprawled over my desk, knocking my things onto the floor with a clatter.

Peter fell on me when my chair couldn't go any further as it jammed against the wall. "You fucker! Where's the damn phone?" he growled, spit hitting my face as I struggled with the weight of him. I tried to get my breath to shout.

There were loud shouts and what sounded like a scuffle before a loud bang. I caught a blur of movement and then Peter flew through the air to land on the outside of my desk. Light-headed, I tried to get the white flashes to stop blinding me, then there was nothing.

~/~/~/~

Cracking open one eye, I shut it fast when the room spun unpleasantly.

"Matty? Pumpkin, sweet boy, can you open your eyes again?"

Positive it was only one eye I'd opened, I chose not to argue when my mind got with the programme and pieced together the events that caused me to pass out cold.

Gentle fingers stroked over my hair and I moved into the touch, assured it was Weston and not Peter by taking a deep breath of Weston's aftershave.

I braved opening my eyes and Weston was right there above me, pale and drawn looking. "Oh baby," he came closer and placed a soft kiss on my forehead. "I'm so sorry I didn't get to you quicker." His voice was thick with emotion, and it was then I realized I was lying on the floor of my office.

How long had I been out of it for?

"Aren't we all," Shaw said from somewhere in the room, causing me to groan when I lifted to look past Weston at the man frowning at me.

I'd gone and made a spectacle of myself at work. This was not good. If I'd thought things were bad before, I could now see me getting my backside fired because surely Peter had made up some bullshit while I'd been out of it.

There was no sign of him in the room as I scanned it, only the mess he'd made. I noticed the door was open and people were milling around outside. I lay back down and shut my eyes, hoping the whole mess was just a nightmare and I'd wake up in a second to find myself in bed, sprawled over Weston.

"Do you think we need to call for paramedics?" Again, this was my boss.

"No, I'm fine," I answered quickly, considering if getting up would give the folks nosing something more to talk about as I'd need to address the monkey in the room—me. "I got the air knocked out of me," I murmured, taking the opportunity to look directly at Weston and gauge a reaction to that. I clearly recall me shouting at him to help before Peter got his hands on me. "It just made me a little lightheaded and I fainted, is all."

"You were out cold, Pumpkin." The set of Weston's jaw made it easy to determine his annoyance.

"Not for long." I hoped that was the case, but without checking the time, I had no real clue.

"I'll deal with this situation with Peter." Shaw moved so he was now close enough that I could see his trouser legs and I decided being on the floor was a definite disadvantage when dealing with this.

"You know my thoughts on this," Weston answered, before I could decide on who to ask what he meant.

Confused, I took the hand Weston offered me to help me stand up. Everything waved for a brief moment, then righted itself. "What thoughts?" It was easy to see I'd missed something vital while I'd been out of it at the look that passed between both men.

"Sit down Matty, please?"

At Shaw's request, I took my seat with Weston right at the side of me, a hand resting on my shoulder. "Are you going to fire me?"

"What... no. Why would you think that?" Shaw rested his backside against the desk in front of me, his gaze traveling over the debris on the floor, frowning.

"The meeting... Peter... this..." I waved my hand around the office like that should explain everything.

"I think you should go home, take tomorrow off, and we'll discuss this on Wednesday." Not one to be smiley, Shaw gave me what looked more like a grimace than a smile. Only the lips curving up at the edges suggested it was an actual smile.

"So you aren't firing me?" I asked, just to be clear, as what was happening didn't really make any sense when I'd no clue where the heck Peter was and how Weston had gotten here so fast.

"Your job is safe. Now go home and rest."

Weston appeared to take Shaw at his word because he bundled me into my coat and, to my mortification, carried me out of the building to his car, leaving the office a mess. I waited until we were driving away to ask what was most prominent in my mind.

"What happened to Peter?" It was easy to remember Weston's threat now I wasn't the center of attention in front of my colleagues.

"He'll get dealt with. He will not bother you again." Absolutely nothing about the reply suggested he wasn't deadly serious.

The worry about my job took a backseat to the jittery oddness going on inside me. Had Weston hit Peter after he got him off me? How did I feel about that?

A flare of desire was the most inappropriate reaction. Wasn't it? "Deal, how?"

My legs squeezed together at the light in Weston's eyes when they left the road briefly to look in my direction.

"In a way that makes him fully understand that coming anywhere near you will result in far worse than what he got today. Now, do I need to go via the emergency room to get you checked out?"

"I fainted. I'm fine, just a little fuzzy around the edges. Nothing some food and bath won't fix."

One check of his expression and I suspected I was going to the emergency room if Weston wasn't satisfied.

Chapter Seventeen

Weston

As I saw it, I was to blame for this mess. Instead of discussing Peter's obvious reasons for escalation with Matty and alerting him to potential problems, I'd avoided it in favor of living in the bubble of my apartment on the weekend.

How did that work out, asshole?

I bit the inside of my cheek to keep the string of curse words to myself. Throughout the day's work, I'd been on a high with how the weekend had turned out. With Matty at the forefront of my thoughts and not wanting to wait until the next day like we'd arranged, I'd driven to his work, planning to ask him out to dinner.

The 'what if' questions had charged through my mind like a herd of buffalo. What if I'd made other plans? What if I'd not been close by? What if Peter had really hurt Matty? What if Matty's boss didn't sack the asshole? They plagued me, causing me to go back over Matty's answer to my question.

"I'll check you over when we get home and if I'm not happy, we're going to the hospital. No arguments, Pumpkin." It was impossible now I had Matty with me and safe to keep all my emotions contained.

I'd been running on pure adrenaline since the call Matty had made to me while I was walking up to his office building to surprise him. It had been me who'd gotten the surprise, an awful one that I was positive would give me nightmares for the coming days. The fear in his voice as he shouted out, 'Daddy, help me' froze me to the bone.

Fear had driven me to race through the building, using the receptionist's directions while I listened to the call hearing crashing and Peter swearing, imagining the worst. Matty's question about what I'd done to Peter was easy to answer, not enough in my opinion, but telling him that wasn't an option when it might scare him. Peter didn't have any obvious marks on him, perhaps. He'd maybe never recover the use of his right arm with how I'd jabbed my fingers into the brachial plexus, aiming for his radial nerve.

It gave little satisfaction to hear him scream with Matty out cold, slumped half in the chair. It was only Matty's boss's arrival that prevented me from doing more. The quick explanation about what I'd seen got Peter escorted out of the office. As we'd had an audience, I had chosen to ignore that he'd gone blubbering and calling threats, for now. In the meantime, I'd be asking Warner and Austin for a little help to keep tabs on Peter until I could fully address that situation.

Shaw Radford, the managing director of the company Matty worked for, from the brief conversation I'd had with him, didn't seem like a fool, but I would need to check what action was taken against Peter.

For now Matty was going to be spending the night with me, and if he wasn't happy about that, then I'd be camping out on Austin's couch. I didn't care where I slept, I just wasn't prepared to let Matty out of my sight. I hoped like hell he wouldn't argue with me, not with the image of his frightened face when I'd come into his office to find him pinned in his chair fresh in my mind.

"This isn't the way back to my house."

My fingers tightened on the steering wheel. "No, I want to take you back to my place." I glanced briefly at him, giving a pleading expression. "Please, I need to make sure you're okay... safe."

Needing to look back at the traffic, I glanced away from his sad face. "Okay, Daddy."

Tension released, making my shoulder blades slip back into place as I breathed a sigh of relief. "Thank you, Pumpkin."

The radio played low and broke the silence that descended between us as I navigated the evening traffic. He remained pensively silent, his brows drawn together, when I parked up, during the ride in the elevator and into the apartment where I switched on the lamps.

He stood in the middle of the room, looking lost and increasing the guilt I was carrying. This morning he'd been smiley and giggly, now...

"Did I do the wrong thing by calling you?" he asked tentatively.

"Gods no," I exclaimed, swooping him up into my arms, wanting to wrap him up and keep him safe from the dangers in the world more than I wanted my next breath. "I put you at risk. I'm to blame for this situation."

My confession got a deep frown. "What? Why? How? You didn't date Peter!" he nestled his cheek against me, rubbing his smooth skin against my whiskers. "And it's Peter's fault really, for being greedy."

"No, I didn't and yes, he was a greedy fuck who wanted his cake and to eat it, too. But I knew he was escalating and blaming you for the situation he's found himself in with Richard. If I'd mentioned it over the weekend, warned you instead of avoiding the topic, then it could have prevented this situation."

He was shaking his head, his arms winding tight around my neck as I held him close, needing contact regardless of the fact the apartment was warm and my coat too thick to wear inside. "Peter is an A hole, Daddy. He wasn't going to listen to anyone 'cause he thinks he knows best. I should have paid more attention and made sure I wasn't alone after he took potshots at me in the last meeting."

I could see we were going to go around in circles and nothing he had to say was going to change my mind. As his Daddy, it was my responsibility to take care of him. I said as much, and he nodded solemnly. "That's why I rang you, Daddy, and you came to look after me." He gave me a head tilt and a shy look that melted my heart. "So you see, you *did* take care of me."

"I suppose we could look at it like that," I skeptically replied.

His lips curled into a cute grin. "And as I fainted with the shock, I'm thinking you need to continue taking care of me with maybe..." he nuzzled my cheek, "sugary treats. That's how you treat shock," he said earnestly.

Laughter rumbled through my chest at the oh-so innocent look that followed the request for sweets. I kissed him, unable to resist the pouty mouth. "And where did you hear that?"

He laid his cheek against mine once more, giggling. "Everyone knows that's how you treat shock, Daddy."

And just like that, everything in my world was as it should be. I tightened my hold for a moment, enjoying the little sigh of pleasure he released. "You need proper food first, then Daddy will see what he can find in his cupboards."

"Alrightttt... can I have hot chocolate while I wait for dinner?" Back was the shy smile.

Lips twitching at how he used it against me, I replied, "No, but you can have some juice in the new sippy cup I bought you."

His squeal and wiggle got me putting him down to watch him dart for the kitchen, where I'd left the open parcels that had arrived before I'd gone to work that morning. The pink cup was metal, with bat-eared foxes on the body and a fox nose spout. It was as cute as the man who was oohing and aahing over it.

"I need to wash it first, but why don't you check through the other parcels?" In the gifts for him were a dinner set that had Mr. Tod, the fox in Beatrice Potter's books, on it. I'd ordered a collection of books, too.

He took off his coat and absently dropped it onto the stool next to him. It held for a second before slithering to the floor unobserved as he attacked the boxes with the enthusiasm of a child on their birthday. I picked up the coat and put it securely on the back of the chair at the dining table, taking mine off and placing it over Matty's.

A loud squeal came when he pulled out the plate with Mr. Tod on it, bringing a grin to my face when I turned to collect the discarded sippy cup to wash it.

"Oh Daddy, look at how smart Mr. Tod looks in his little coat and red waistcoat."

I glanced down at the plate, easily getting caught up with his enthusiasm. "He does. Should we honor him by having a tea party? You could invite Gaines, too." Walking to the sink to wash the cup, the sound of water hitting the sink filled the room.

"And Terrence?" he questioned.

When it registered who he meant, I nodded agreement. "Of course, if that's what you want."

He placed the plate down ever so carefully on the side by my elbow, skipping on the spot, flushed with happiness. Any telltale signs of the trauma he'd been through earlier with Peter seemed forgotten.

"Terrence has invited me to play lots of times. I could show off my playroom." His lower lip got sucked into his mouth and his expression softened. "We can have playtime here, can't we, Daddy? Like a proper playtime with Daddies and their boys. We could all squeeze into my bed. Can we, pleaseeeee?"

Picking up the cloth, I dried my hands before reaching to pinch his chin gently to hold it while I gave him a kiss. His eyes sparkled up at me. "You can, anytime you like."

"You're the bestest Daddy," he sing-songed, puckering up for another kiss. His lips rubbed over mine, then he skipped back to the boxes after he got one. Back to rifling in the boxes, lots of cheerful noises came as I kept busy sorting out dinner.

The meal went by in a flurry as I witnessed him sink into Little space. Softness around his eyes and mouth came first, then the excited, giggly chatter started. By the time I fed him his ice cream with chocolate sauce and sprinkles, he was bouncing on his stool, eager for playtime.

"Be careful, Pumpkin, we don't want you falling off the chair onto the ground."

His brow furrowed and his lips pinched together, the scowl as adorable as him. "I already did that 'cause of Peter, but I never hurt my bottom. Daddy swooped in to save me like a superhero." His arms lifted in the air, and he made the swoop and dive, nearly knocking the spoon I was holding, which was dripping ice cream over the counter.

"Daddy isn't that. And careful, Pumpkin, we don't want to make a mess."

His smile was pure mischief. Before I could figure out his intentions, he tipped the spoon and opened his mouth, only catching half. The rest dribbled down his chin and onto the button-down white shirt.

"Oops..." His giggles erupted as he licked around his mouth chasing the chocolate, smearing brown goo everywhere, while he half heartedly rubbed at his shirt, making a right mess as the chocolate continued to drip off his chin.

It was impossible to hold back my amusement when the cheeky imp was having fun. "Oops... really?" I arched my brow, aiming for stern and failing miserably when I choked on my laughter. "Pumpkin, are you being naughty?"

Wide, round, innocent eyes stared back at me. "Nooo. I was trying to help Daddy by eating what was on the spoon." He shrugged and looked at his hand, then his shirt. "'Cept some of it missed my mouth."

"Helping, I see. It looks like I'll need to give you a bath before we have playtime." I came forward at the urge to be playful and licked at his chin, tasting the sweet mixture.

More giggles erupted from him when I pulled back.

"Daddy's messy too." He dived at me, and I caught him by dropping the spoon with a clatter, laughing as I rocked to standing to prevent us both from falling.

At the feeling of his sticky hands clasping around my neck, I groaned. They went into my short hair, clinging on. His body was shaking with his laughter as I got sticky kisses scattered over my face as a reward. "Yep, you're my superhero, Daddy."

More laughter resulted as he tried to come up with a superhero name for me when I carried him through to the bathroom to run the bath. "Sugar Daddy? No. Ice cream Daddy? No, I don't like that either."

His little nose scrunched up after several more attempts at finding a name he liked. As I turned off the taps, I straightened up and then wiped my hands on a towel.

"Super strength Daddy," I suggested as I stood him up to strip off his clothes, doing my best to unbutton the shirt and not dirty my now clean hands.

"Ooh 'cause when you were at the gym playing ball, you were super strong?"

"Yes, like that," I answered, distracted as I crouched to tug his skinny legged trousers down.

"Can you do other exercises using me to help?" His hands rested on my shoulders without asking and I could hear the change in his tone, suggesting he was coming out of Little space.

I encouraged him to lift his foot, taking his shoe and sock off before slipping the leg of his trousers off. "I suppose so. There are potentially lots of ways I could use you to exercise," I answered, more focused on getting his clothes off.

When I reached for his briefs, his cock was tenting the front of the fabric, making me wonder exactly where his thoughts had gone at my reply. I moved my attention to the upper part of his body, grinning. "You got something on your mind, Pumpkin?"

A rosy glow coated his chest, neck, and the parts of his face not smeared with chocolate sauce. "What ways could you use me?"

Taking in his lack of attire, I seriously considered the things I could do using him. The dragonfly challenge sprang to mind, and I considered the available space on the bathroom floor and the rug on it versus the carpet in my bedroom. "Maybe you could act as my dumbbell for the dragon fly challenge?"

"Dragon fly challenge," he asked breathlessly. "What's that?"

I left his briefs on for now, resisting the temptation of holding his naked ass and potentially distracting myself with what I considered doing. I rose to stand, my hands going to the buttons of my shirt.

Dilated pupils tracked my movements as Matty's chest rose and fell in quick succession, his eyes hawklike as I removed my clothing. Fastidious to a fault, I picked up everything and placed it all in the hamper, leaving just my boxer briefs on. Grabbing a washcloth, I dipped it in the bath water then wiped Matty's chin and hands to get rid of the stickiness.

Hands dried and towel draped on the side of the bath, I reached for his now clean hand. "Let me show you."

I encouraged him out of the steamy family bathroom and down the corridor to my bedroom. Keeping my wicked grin to myself, I eyed the space at the bottom on the bed, to calculate how much room I'd need.

Dropping his hand, I walked over the carpet, doing several stretches to warm my muscles, then lay down. Getting comfortable, I signaled for him to come to me from where he'd remained standing by the door, watching me closely as his cock poked at his underwear.

Arms stretched over my head, I grinned at him when I caught him staring at my body. "Okay, I need you to come and place that pert little ass in my hands."

He blinked slowly, as if trying to get his brain to get with the programme. "Won't that be a bit heavy and awkward?"

"Not if you imagine using my hands like the seat of a chair. I need you to cross your legs and use your hands to hold them to keep them as close to your body and off the ground. I'll use your body weight as an anchor of sorts, the same way I'd use a dumbbell to keep my upper body anchored to the floor."

Frowning but not questioning me further, he made sure not to stand on my arms and lowered his ass into the palms of my hands. Looking back was impossible at this angle, so I kept my head on the ground, waiting for him to cross his legs and get sorted.

His small ass flexing in the palm of my hands sent bolts of desire to other parts of my body that would give Matty much more of a show once I got started. "You ready?"

"I think so. But I don't know what you'r—"

He ceased talking abruptly when I used his body as a counter-weight, contracting my lower body and placing my legs together. I brought them up first, then my hips and lower back up off the floor until only my shoulders and head were touching the ground. Then I brought Matty up, my arms off the ground until he was floating above my face. In one fluid move, every muscle in my body strained as I lowered him and my legs back towards the carpet, neither touching. They hovered inches from the ground before my abs rippled and I repeated the move, lifting Matty and my lower body up. I held on to my core, working to breathe through the move, sweat slicking my skin by the third repetition.

The ass in my hands squeezed tight as I heard a low groan from above me. With the effort required to breathe, never mind talk, all I could do was listen to the litany of breathy noises that came from Matty. Each sound aided in perking up my arousal, which I was sure he was staring at when my body arched once more, my legs aiming for the ceiling, once again putting Matty within touching distance of my cock.

The next groan was all me at the fingers stroking over my straining cock in my boxer briefs. Straining to hold him with the bolts of electricity coming from his touch, I ungracefully hit the carpet.

Chapter Eighteen

Matty

The show of strength and the hard cock protruding from the band of his underwear, it was all too much. High as a kite at the visual in front of me, I lost the battle to touch with the scent of Weston warming the air.

Thumping to the carpet, Weston groaned.

"Sorry," I mumbled, intent on getting closer to what I wanted. Playing at the gym with Weston in front of an audience and doing this alone in his bedroom was totally different.

"So okay, Pumpkin," he stated breathlessly.

Heart thundering hard enough to make me shake with how turned on I was, I unfolded my legs to place them on either side of his arms. I came forward, crawling down his sweat slicked body. I slid over warm, quivering muscles until my knees hit his shoulders. My sights were on the hardness that was peaking out at me. Hands in the elastic of his underwear, his moan vibrated through my balls as his mouth touched me right as I felt his velvety hardness.

Reaching my mouth watering goal, I licked at the head of the glistening cock that tasted slightly bitter. My fingers tugged eagerly at the pants, pushing them under his balls, which caused his cock to come closer to me. Thick and veiny, the silver hair at the base was springy and soft when I ran my fingers through it to cup him. My fingers were not long enough to go around the girth, causing me to groan at thoughts of how he'd feel when he was inside me.

"Suck Daddy," he mouthed against my balls, his hot breath dampening the fabric of my underwear. A hand moved between my legs, moving the fabric of my underwear to one side, exposing my balls to Weston's mouth.

Legs quivering, I shuddered, angling his cock to lick around the flared head, looking for where the foreskin was attached. I nibbled on the knot of flesh, getting rewarded by more suction on my balls. Pulses of pleasure danced down my spine and it was hard to remember what I was doing, let alone my name.

The cock between my parted lips thrust a little deeper into my mouth, reminding me of what I was doing. I widened my lips and sucked him deeper, holding on to the base to stop myself from choking on his length. Pre-come coated my tongue as I ran it around the head, teasing and tasting, lapping up all his essence.

Weston showed his appreciation, moaning and groaning. Tiny vibrations skittered up my spine, and I rocked into him, looking for friction on my cock while sucking harder on his.

Spit slid over his cock and down over my fingers as I moved up and down his length, seeking every bit of pre-cum. His dick pulsed and thickened. The head hit the back of my throat, causing me to ease off a little as I coughed. My hips rocked when the body beneath me stiffened. I jabbed my tongue into his slit as the first ribbon of cum spilled into my willing mouth. I groaned in delight, sucking down every drop that spurted onto my tongue.

At the release of my balls, a complaint rose in my throat, only for it to turn to a moan when Weston's tongue slid over my hole, making me lose my rhythm. His tongue ran over the sensitive flesh repeatedly, bathing it in warm, wet heat.

At the desperate aching need for more, I pushed my ass closer to his face and clenched my hole on the tongue jabbing at me. His chuckle ran through the tight rim of muscle, leaving me with flutters in my ass that gave me an empty feeling.

"Daddyyyy," I complained around the softening cock in my mouth, cum dripping out of the corner of my lips as I pointlessly cast a glance over my shoulder, knowing Weston couldn't see me. The achy feeling grew at the lack of touch on my cock.

Hands came through my legs and cupped my ass, pulling my cheeks apart, stretching open my ass. His tongue stroked over the wet skin, up the crease, and to the back of my balls. Once, twice, three times before he circled my hole. I pushed down, hoping to feel the burn of his tongue penetrating me when it disappeared.

A quick swat to my ass cheek, then he squeezed my ass wide again. "Daddy's in charge," he growled huskily.

Where the swat had landed, the skin warmed, adding to the torture as the tongue went back to long, lazy sweeps up and down my crease, barely quelling the growing ball of need forming at the base of my spine. Sweating hard at trying to stop myself from impaling myself on his tongue, my eyes screwed shut as I released his cock, panting hard, bracing against his hard muscles.

Barely seconds later, it was too much, and I wailed, "Ooh... please... more... I'll be good... just need... more!"

I cried out as the tongue pushed deep into my ass and cum spurted out my cock with enough force to make it throb and my ass to clamp down on the appendage currently sending me to outer space. Each spasm stronger than the next, they held me hostage in an out of control spiral of desire, a place I never wanted to leave.

Resting my sweaty cheek on Weston's stomach, I chugged in deep breaths, trying to gain back some semblance of control. Only it was useless with how all the energy in my body disappeared with the cum coating the insides of my underwear.

One dominant thought seeped into my awareness. What had the potential to be a disaster of an evening, because of the man beneath me, had changed. Weston had wiped away the bad and left only fuzzy feelings of serenity. It was fast becoming the only way I wanted to feel. Weston's ability to make me forget all the bad stuff—which was a rare ability in my experience—was like a superpower.

Weston shifted beneath me, and I realized too late my balls were probably trying to suffocate him. "Have you fallen asleep on me?"

He sounded amused as I shook my head, then realized he couldn't see me. "No, Daddy. I'm just waiting for my brain cells to recall what day it is and who I am."

Warm chuckles hit the inside of my thigh. "As much as I love this position, the floor isn't the most comfortable place to have a nap."

"You're very comfy to lie on, Daddy." I snuggled in and inhaled the musky scent of him.

"That may be so, but Daddy much prefers his bed with you sprawling all over me. And if you have forgotten, I was about to give you a bath."

"Daddy, you'll need to carry me. I'm all wobbly," I mumbled from a lack of energy, really wanting to take a nap right where I was.

"Don't fall asleep, Pumpkin." Hands moved up to my hips and lifted them until my lower body was at a right angle, pushing my head more into Weston's stomach. "I need you to help me, just for a moment, then I'll carry you."

Grumbling, I followed his instructions and wedged my upper body up using the floor as he lifted me high enough over his head, getting me to hold my legs close to my body so as not to clout him with a stray foot. Somehow, a minute later, he was standing, and we were both minus our underwear and heading back to the bathroom.

Steam covered the mirror and the tiles glistened wetly as he tested the water before reaching for the tap to add more hot water. He perched me on his hip and I rested my head on his shoulder, watching him with heavy eyes. He checked the water temperature before turning off the tap.

An adoring smile that made my heart flutter came with a brush of lips over mine. "Hold on to my neck and tuck up your feet towards your bottom, Pumpkin."

Doing as he asked, he stepped into the water and carefully lowered into the hot, scented water. The joy of the huge bath meant I didn't have to let go, and I groaned at the brush of wet skin sliding over mine as I let my legs stretch back out, coming to rest on top of Weston. My back complained for a moment at the overextended arch until Weston lay down fully and placed his head on the bath pillow. He encouraged me to rest my head on the top of his chest where the water didn't quite reach. His hands gently stroked up and down my spine as the scent of mint and lavender wafted up on the rising steam. "Sooo... goodddd," I murmured, eyelids struggling to stay open.

He brushed a kiss over my forehead. "Then Daddy did his job properly."

I opened my eyes, which had drifted shut, at the seriousness of Weston's tone, tilting my head to look at him. What I saw there in the depth of his gaze made my heart jolt into my throat.

"Everything you do makes me feel so special." I puckered up for a kiss, loving the slow smile that came as he lifted his head for a better angle. Lips brushed over mine, light as a feather, teasing before he sucked my lower lip into his mouth and bit gently. A hum of desire warmed me but didn't combat my exhaustion. His hands cupped my ass, and the kiss deepened, his tongue seeking entry, stroking inside my mouth, savoring me. It was how he always made me feel.

He rested his head back on the bath and reached for the bar of soap. He ran it over my skin, not rushing, just a slippery guide until every muscle in my body felt they had no solid substance left.

Utter bliss the kind I never wanted to stop. Something I was fast coming to realize that Weston could achieve easily, making him addictive.

~/~/~/~

Distinct sounds of voices coming from the kitchen, as I exited the bedroom dressed in the clothes I'd worn the day before, drew me down the hallway. The laundered clothes revealed just how long Weston had been up while I'd slept in. I'd been shocked to see it was after ten on what should have been a workday. I only ever slept in on a weekend and rarely on a weekday, even when on vacation.

I paused at the female voice, second guessing whether I should reveal I was there. I decided to poke my head around the door fast enough to assess who was there and allow for a retreat.

"There you are, Pumpkin," Weston said, the second my head appeared around the door frame. I froze when the woman sitting at the center kitchen island swiveled around on her seat, aiming her attention at me. Two things struck at once; the similarities between her and Weston, and that she looked young enough that surely she could be mistaken for Weston's sister. As he didn't have any siblings, I had to surmise she was, in fact, his mom.

"Hey... I can see you've got company, so I'll head off."

A deep crease appeared between Weston's brows and his lips parted, but it was his mom that spoke first.

"I'm not company, just his mom, but you can call me Nina." Up off the seat, she walked to me as I continued to hover by the door, looking between her and Weston, who continued to frown at me. Dressed casually in a lemon jumper and jeans, the silver hair framing her face hung in a perfect bob as she held out her hand. "Nice to meet you, Matty. My son was telling me all about you. Only he failed to mention just how pretty you are. I'm so envious of your curls."

Feeling awkward, I reached out a hand to her, only she ignored it and gave me a big hug, the kind that Weston was so good at. I looked over her shoulder at Weston, noticing she was as small as me. His lips twitched as I gave him a 'please help me' look, which he shrugged off.

"You must be hungry. What do you want on your pancakes, Pumpkin?"

Released from the hug, Nina grinned and took my hand to tug me towards the seat she'd vacated. "Pumpkin? Why do you call him that? He's not orange or round." Her laughter was bold and friendly as she sat, picking up a cup which smelled like it contained coffee.

A blush coated his cheeks, fascinating me with why he'd become embarrassed about the yet unknown reason he called me that name. Taking the seat next to Nina, I grinned cheekily at him, liking his mom. "Yes, why do you call me Pumpkin?"

He shook his head, eyeing the pair of us. "Mom, really? Matty don't encourage her. If you give her an inch, she'll take a mile."

Giggling, I rested my chin on my knuckles after placing my elbows on the counter, watching him pull out a plate of pancakes from the warmer. "It was a simple question, D... Weston."

It was my turn to blush at the near slip up but, quickly glancing at Nina, it seemed she didn't notice. I let slip a little sigh of relief as she sipped at her coffee, appearing relaxed.

I recalled Weston had mentioned Nina knew he was gay, just not about the kink he was into, so I gave him an apologetic smile. The slight head shake, and remaining smile ensured the knot wanting to form in my stomach didn't get a chance.

"Come on son, why?"

"Mom!" he said, all exasperation, but with some apparent amusement. "If you must know, when I met Matty back in August, he was in the park talking to himself and I wanted to check he was okay."

At his pause, Nina tilted her head and winked at me. "And?"

He huffed, making me struggle not to laugh at the antics of the pair of them. "He looked as sweet as your pumpkin pie, the one you make for my birthday, because *I love it* so much."

At the mention of love, I lost my sense of humor when he stressed how much he loved it. Were the powerful feelings he'd talked about having for me—love?

Hyperventilating with how easy it was for me to think along those lines when he was everything I'd dreamed of having as a boyfriend, a daddy, and possibly a future husband, I tried to force myself to calm down.

Stop jumping the gun! Stop it.

"Why, what a lovely compliment." She placed her cup down and went to Weston, wrapping her arms around his middle, not tall enough to reach for his shoulders, and hugged him hard. "But that won't get you out of trouble for not mentioning you've been dating for over three months and never told me!"

Chapter Nineteen

Weston

My heaved sigh said everything about how I was feeling at being caught out by Mom. She was better than a police dog sniffing out drugs when it came to getting information. That I'd forgotten she was coming this morning for breakfast was testament to the man sitting next to her, looking poleaxed at my confession to why I call him pumpkin.

"What do you want on your pancakes?" I asked again, using that as an excuse to give me a little breathing room. I was happy for Mom to meet Matty, just maybe not right now, when it might lead to questions as to why Matty wasn't at work.

"Chocolate and strawberries," he replied, watching Mom as she came back around the counter to sit next to him, her expression very revealing. I scrambled to come up with something to distract her from what was coming.

"Chocolate for breakfast?" I arched a brow, causing him to squirm, even when he nodded enthusiastically, giving Mom the side eye.

"Pancakes need chocolate and I'm having fruit, too. That's healthy," he pointed out, giving me an angelic look.

It was wrong to even hope I'd avoided the questions when I set the plate in front of Matty, having chopped strawberries and coated each pancake in chocolate, not considering the care I took in preparing the food. Matty continued to explain how chocolate was a bean and therefore classed as a staple food group, entertaining Mom for the time being.

He didn't wait more than a second to dive into the food and the silence gave Mom the opening she was waiting for.

"So, when were you going to tell me you were dating, hmm?" Cup in hand, she held my stare over the rim. "Did you plan for Matty to be here this morning so we could meet?"

Matty coughed as he swallowed a piece of strawberry, his gaze remaining on the plate in front of him, hunching over it.

"No..." truth was always best, despite the narrow-eye stare I was now getting. "We met in August in the park that I like to jog in. And it was a kind of causal thing to start with." I was failing epically in explaining myself when Matty finally fixed his attention on me, his lower lip trembling before he clamped it between his teeth. "Shit! I don't mean it like that."

It appeared to be my turn to go around the counter. I took the fork from Matty's hand and placed it down before scooping him up in my arms.

Kissing him, he tasted of the sweetness from the strawberries and chocolate. It took a moment, but his arms crept around my neck as his legs dangled down with my hands under his bottom, holding him up. "There is nothing casual about how I feel about you. That first time in the park when you didn't see me, I couldn't take my eyes off you. Those couple of missing weeks you weren't in the park, I ran several times those days just in case you came by later," I confessed.

"Really?"

"That's my cue to leave, I think."

The hands around my neck tightened briefly before they let go. "No, you don't have to leave." Matty offered Mom a genuine smile as he wiggled to get down. "If you go, I'll never know what he might confess to next."

"Cheeky boy," I murmured, giving him a quick peck before putting him back on his seat.

"Yep." Not looking at all upset now, he picked the fork back up and stabbed at a sizable piece of pancake, pushing it into his mouth, smearing chocolate over his lips and bringing back the memory of the night before. The cheeky imp licked at his lips in such a way it suggested he knew exactly where my head had gone.

Mom, not one to let anything go, got right back to interfering. "So what are you doing for Thanksgiving, Matty?"

He peeked at me, chewing slowly and swallowing. "Usually I celebrate with my best friend Gaines. We live together. My parents travel at this time of year, so they're rarely here for the holidays."

"Oh, that's a shame. Are they away for Christmas too?"

Despite the obvious concern at Matty being alone for the holidays, I gave Mom a stern look. "Mom, please stop fishing. Matty, what my mom wants to know is, do you want to spend Thanksgiving with us this year?"

"I wasn't fishing, just encouraging you to ask him," she answered self-assuredly, not looking at all abashed for pushing me.

"I'd love to." His cheeks were pink and glowing as he accepted my offer, making me grin at the culprit who had started the conversation.

Mom settled more on her seat and twisted to look at Matty when I went over to clean up the countertop of the remnants from Matty's breakfast. "So what do you do for a living Matty? Weston hadn't gotten around to telling me that?"

My groan got lost as Matty answered. "I work for Product Development Technologies. I do product design for them."

He explained a little about what he did and enlightened me further into how stressful his job actually was with the expansion of the company through the States and beyond. Particularly when I considered what an asshole Peter was and how Matty had remained professional despite him. I, on the other hand, might have considered socking the fucker in the face for being a dick.

"Sounds like you have a very stressful job. Do you only work part time?"

It was a valid question with it being a Tuesday, one I noticed that made Matty wince.

"No, I work full time. My boss gave me a day off today." Back to hunching over his plate, Mom turned her attention to me, giving me an enquiring look I didn't miss.

"Matty had a minor issue yesterday and his boss felt an additional day off was warranted," I explained, without giving much away.

"Which means I get the bonus of getting an unexpected day with my boyfriend."

Mom, knowing me as she did, understood my tone of voice, which suggested we should drop the subject. "How lovely. Do you have something in mind?"

I did, but I didn't want to spoil the surprise. Having got up at my normal time, I'd had time to sort Matty's clothes, call Austin about the events with Peter, then do some internet searches for up-and-coming dates with the festive season fast approaching. I loved the festive lights at Brookfield Zoo, which started around Thanksgiving time, and they gave me the idea to buy tickets for Lincoln zoo today. It would be the perfect place to spend the afternoon with an unexpected day off. "Yep, but it's a secret."

Matty sat up straight. "A secret, oohhh, what are we doing?"

"Secrets, Pumpkin," I reached over and tweaked his nose, making him grin, "are more fun when they remain that."

"You two are adorable."

I glanced at Mom and rolled my eyes. "Please, I'm forty-four years old. How can I be adorable?"

She picked up her cup and Matty's now empty plate and got off the stool before going to the sink. "You'll always be my baby. Now I think it is time I left." Dishes washed, she left them on the drainer, picking up the towel I'd used earlier to wipe her hands. "It was lovely to meet you, Matty, and I'll look forward to seeing you again at Thanksgiving."

"Do you need me to bring anything?" Matty glanced at me, mischief there for me to see. "Pumpkin pie, maybe?"

Mom slapped me on my arm as she passed, laughing as she went to retrieve her coat. "I like him." To Matty, she shook her head. "No, I make enough to feed forty thousand. Just bring an appetite."

In a flurry of kisses and goodbyes, Mom left like she always did in a whirlwind of hugs and promises to make sure I didn't forget to visit her.

Matty, who'd got up to accept the hug, stood next to me, staring at the now closed door. "Is she always like that?"

"Pretty much, you'll get used to her... *possibly*."

"I should warn you, my parents are a lot more reserved, so when you meet them, don't expect the warm affection of your mom. They could take lessons from her."

He said it so simplistically, I had to stop for a second to assess whether or not he was upset by that fact. There was nothing to say he was. The smile reached his eyes, so I nodded.

"Warning taken. When do I get to meet your folks?" I enquired causally, guiding him to the chair where I'd left the coats the evening before.

"They leave for a two-month cruise at the beginning of next week. I was planning to visit this coming Sunday and do brunch with them, if you want to come with me?"

The impression of his stillness suggested he was waiting for a rejection. "I'd love to. How about you stay here for the weekend, then we could go together? We could see if Gaines and Terrence are free on Saturday for a Littles party?"

I staggered, coats in hand, as he pounced at me, doing his best to reach up on his tiptoes to kiss me. He barely reached my chin, so it was more miss than hit with the kisses. "Can we really? Oh, Daddy! I'm so excited," he squealed hard enough to hurt my eardrums.

I gave up and dropped the coats, catching him up in my arms so I could receive the kisses he was desperately trying to give me. "We can. Daddy will shop and get things to make a proper tea party and we can use your Mr. Tod plates."

That got more squealing and kisses, so it took a while longer to get out the door with coats on and my wallet, keys and cell phone tucked in my pocket. Out of the building and in the car headed to Lincoln Park zoo, Matty didn't stop his excited chatter while he texted Gaines and Terrence to invite them over.

"They said yes! Although Gaines is mad at me for not letting him know I wasn't coming home last night." He gave a heartfelt moan. "He's going to lose it when I tell him about Peter."

I'd spent a while considering how to keep Peter as far away from Matty as possible. "I spoke to Austin this morning about the situation yesterday. Between us all, we'll ensure he has no ability to come anywhere near you again." That included work, and though that might be trickier if Shaw didn't fire his ass, I had faith in Austin and Warner to assist with the shithead. "Do you want me to ask Austin to talk to Gaines for you?"

The only sound in the car was the radio playing quietly for several seconds. It was tempting to try and fill the silence but I held myself, gripping the steering wheel tighter as I navigated the mid-morning traffic.

"Do you think Peter will try to hurt me?" he asked instead.

The quietly spoken question cut at my heart when there was a definite quiver in his voice. "He won't get the opportunity to come anywhere near you again."

"How can you be so sure? We don't know how Shaw will deal with Peter. I know he said I wasn't going to lose my job, but I can't see him firing Peter either 'cause it's got nothing to do with his ability to do his job."

It was a hard one to call and I didn't want to give Matty false hope where Peter was concerned. The only guarantee I could give was that Peter would not get close enough to Matty to lay a finger on him again. When Matty returned to work the next day, I would have another private chat with Shaw to explain my feelings on the subject of protecting my boy while he was in that damn building. "Do you trust me?"

"Yes." At the lack of hesitation, my chest swelled with affection.

"Then know this, I will do everything in my power to keep you safe no matter where you are." One quick glance at Matty, who was staring at me, showed he understood I was serious. It was hard not to reach over and kiss him at that moment.

He reached over and placed a hand on my thigh, squeezing. "I believe you, Daddy."

"Good," I managed to choke out past the ball of emotion firmly lodged in my throat.

"Daddy, are you going to tell me where we're going?"

The change of topic was welcome and after swallowing twice to clear my throat, I answered, "A place you love."

"Really? I love lots of places. You aren't being fair, Daddy." He made a sound that was a cross between a huffy breath and a put-upon sigh.

"Come on, don't you like to play guessing games?" My lips twitched as he crossed his arms and flopped in his seat.

"I was never good at guessing games," he complained, sounding very much like a sullen teenager.

"What if I give you a reward for each guess you make?"

Instantly, he perked up. "I like rewards."

After another quick glance at him, I noticed he was paying more attention to where we were. "Think about what you love the most."

His giggle was naughty, and I'd have given anything to read his mind when he didn't enlighten me as to where his thoughts had gone.

"Pumpkin, are you having wicked thoughts?"

"Possibly... but I'm not telling 'cause I want to know if I get to choose my rewards for guessing?"

That was easy, he could choose whatever he wanted, and I'd do my best to get it for him. "Yes, if you want to."

"Is it a shop we're going to?"

"No."

His hand lifted, and he rubbed his chin. "Is it an inside thing?"

"Parts can be inside."

"Ohhh, I know, I know." He bounced in the seat, only the seatbelt stopping him from moving too much.

"You do. Where are we going?"

"A secret garden?"

I cast a grin at him. "Nope, not a park."

"If it's outside and inside..." his pause came with a loud whoop. "I know, I know. The zoo. It's the zoo. Please say it is."

I couldn't contain my laughter as he tugged at the sleeve of my jacket when I didn't give him an immediate answer. "Yes. See, you are a good guesser."

He looked like he might burst with pride when I slowed to take the next exit and looked at him. "Thanks Daddy. How many guesses did I make?"

"Three? Four?" I replied, distracted by watching the traffic.

"I think it was four. That means I get four rewards."

Nothing particular about the way he said it indicated what was on his mind, yet something triggered my gut, and it fluttered as I finally caught a break and made the turn down the street leading to the zoo. "What rewards do you want?"

He tapped my leg. "Daddy, that's for me to know and you to find out."

Shaking with laughter at his devious tone, I had to work to concentrate and not stare at the boy wiggling his ass in the seat next to me. "Are you challenging, Daddy?"

"Could be…" he came as close as the seatbelt would stretch, "'cause I know my Daddy won't fail me."

Chapter Twenty

Matty

Wednesday morning came around far too fast and though I'd dressed to impress, it didn't stop the anxious gnawing feeling in the pit of my stomach. When I'd gone via the house before coming to work to get clean clothes, Gaines had been waiting for me and pounced the second I was through the door. He'd been emotional, and it explained why Austin was still home. There hadn't been time to explain every-thing, not with two hovering Daddies. I'd promised Gaines I'd talk to him tonight when I got home. I would also know more about what was going on with Peter.

The day before had made it really easy to forget all my worries. Weston was the best distraction in the world. He left me with no time to stress and visiting the zoo was a perfect way to just be myself. Right now, regardless of the fact he was right with me as I walked into work, my head was all up in how many colleagues had seen me lying on the floor of my office. What had they gossiped about while I'd had the day off?

"It's going to be fine," Weston bent and whispered in my ear as I didn't acknowledge anyone, heading to my boss's office where his text last night requested I meet him.

"I hope so," I murmured back as we approached Shaw's personal assistant, Monica. Dark eyes lifted from the desk and revealed none of her thoughts. She'd been Shaw's assistant as long as I'd worked for the company. She didn't tend to be overly friendly with anyone and I wasn't sure if that was because of her job or if she just didn't like folks.

Her hand lifted and pointed to my boss's closed office door. "Good morning, Matty. Shaw said to go straight in." She glanced briefly at Weston but didn't question his presence as he walked ahead of me, knocked on the door before opening it.

"Thank you."

Weston stepped aside and gave me an encouraging smile.

I stood to my full height and walked with as much confidence as I could muster into the large office that overlooked the golf course. Gray skies outside didn't detract from the feeling of warmth in the room. Maroon carpet and walnut furniture graced the elegant space. Every available bit of wall space held pictures of designs the company had created and won awards for, one of which was mine.

The imposing man behind the desk, dressed all in black, didn't initially look up from what he looked to be reading. It gave me a chance to take a breath and walk to the seats opposite his desk and wait. Weston's scent was strong enough to show just how close he was to me, without actually touching me.

When Shaw looked up, he shifted back, relaxing in his chair. His assessing gaze went from me to Weston. He lifted his hand to indicate for us to sit. "Please, sit."

Once we had, he templed his fingers under his chin, his gaze back on me. "How are you feeling today, Matty?"

"To be honest, nervous," I blurted out with no filter and blushed at the narrowed eyes appraising me.

"I suspected you would be." He came forward in his seat, a hand reaching for a pen, which he spun in his fingers in a natural move that suggested he did it a lot. "I'll cut to the chase. I met with Peter yesterday and he'll be transferring to our offices in Austin, Texas."

"He will?" I asked, too shocked to think about waiting to see if Shaw had finished speaking.

"Yes. After an in-depth conversation, the details of which I won't bore you with, I felt it was in Peter's best interest to accept the new position and cease any thoughts of pressing charges—"

I was up off the seat immediately, hands on my hips. "Pressing charges against who? Me? Weston? He was only protecting me. Peter should never have acted the way he did towards me. He's been harassing me for months."

"None of which you informed me of," Shaw pointed out, in a way that made me sink back into the seat at being called out. "I'm a very busy man, but I have an open door policy for staff if they are having any work related issues. This, I would suggest, fits that description. That being said, I met with several staff yesterday before meeting with

Peter, to ascertain what led to the way Peter behaved in the meeting and subsequently in your office. The part where he cheated on you with another member of staff is none of my business. But his harassing and ridiculing you in front of others certainly breaches the ethics code applied to all staff and part of your contract of employment. You could have filed a complaint to HR about his behavior, which is unacceptable. My issue is that you never followed the correct path and tied my hands. Moving Peter to another office after my internal investigation and discussion with my lawyer was the only option open to me."

Weston ran a hand over the sleeve of my jacket, then interlaced our fingers. "When does Peter leave?"

"I have given him the week off to organize for the move. He received a formal written warning and is to have no contact with Matty, which he has agreed to."

Every bit of worry at having to face Peter melted away and a bubbly feeling of euphoria came, which was probably inappropriate, but then no one knew but me. Then a thought registered. "What about Richard?"

Just a hint of a smile curled the edges of Shaw's lips, though there was a hard glint in his eyes that could chill the skin when he replied, "Richard is switching offices with Peter. They'll be working together. As they're engaged, it seems wrong to separate them, especially when the move is permanent."

I had no memory of the rest of the conversation when I waltzed out of the room minutes later, clutching Weston's hand. He walked me back to my office and only when the door closed behind us did I do a very inappropriate little dance. Ass wiggling, I bopped about my office, hands in the air, laughing. "Peter hates the heat. Austin, Texas will fry his bottom."

An amused looking Weston came over to me and bent to cup my cheeks, holding me still. "Are you gloating?"

"A little. I shouldn't, it's not nice."

He kissed the tip of my nose. "This once won't harm."

Giggling, I came up on my toes and puckered up for a kiss. "Daddy, you're the best."

Breathless and wishing I was back in Weston's apartment moments later, he stopped kissing me to let me go. "Are you happy for Daddy to leave now?"

"Yes, I am." Turning serious, I stepped back to Weston. "And Daddy, thank you for coming with me this morning. For being such a wonderful man."

Another nose kiss was my reward, and a smile that turned my belly into a haven for buzzing bees. "With you, it's as easy as breathing. I'll be back at five to pick you up and take you back home."

The reminder that I wasn't going back to Weston's tonight left a sour taste in my mouth and a forced smile on my face. Quickly getting Weston out of the office without him noticing my mood change, I leaned against the closed door and stared unseeingly at my office. How had spending four nights in Weston's apartment changed my view of where my home was?

~/~/~/~

I'd barely got my coat off and my jacket down my arms when Gaines was dragging me from the front door and up the stairs away from Weston, who wore a perplexed expression. Deep lines over his forehead hadn't shifted since he'd picked me up and driven me here.

For all Gaines' cuteness, he was strong from pole dancing and wasn't for letting me decide if I wanted to go with him when he tugged and grumbled about me moving my backside quicker. Inside my messy bedroom—the place as I'd left it days earlier and now didn't feel like it once did—I sat on the unmade bed with Gaines next to me. My jacket flung on the bed, I sagged in defeat.

"Spill. What happened with Peter? Did he hit you?" Tears sprung in Gaines' eyes as he wrapped an arm around my shoulders. "If he hurts you, I'll... I'll stick my portable pole up his bottom!"

The watery threat held lots of heat and brought tears to my own eyes. "No, he kind of landed on me trying to get my cell phone when I rang Daddy and asked him to help me get away from Peter."

"Wow, you rang Weston for help? You must really love him!" he exclaimed, so loud I glanced at the closed door hoping Weston hadn't followed and was outside listening.

What happened with Peter now seeming to be of no interest to Gaines or me.

"Isn't it too soon to declare those types of feelings?" I sobbed, unsure why I was crying.

"You're asking me? It was barely weeks after meeting Austin that I knew I loved him. You encouraged me to listen and trust myself. I think when you know, you know." He shrugged and hugged me to his side and I caught the scent of his body wash.

"It's scary 'cause I don't want to be here," I confessed, like I was ripping a plaster off. "It's not that I don't love you. 'cause you know I do, it's just..."

"You want to be with Weston all the time? For him to be your Daddy all the time 'cause he makes you feel good."

Nodding, I rested my head on his shoulder, wiping my damp eyes. "You know, I never really had that before with anyone."

He nodded solemnly.

"The idea of staying here tonight doesn't feel right after spending the last four nights getting to stretch over Daddy's body. He makes everything feel like nothing is too much to deal with. And I'm not gonna lie, he's real comfy to sleep on."

"I bet he is," Gaines said, giggling. "My Daddy is great for curling up on, too."

"What am I gonna do?" I whispered, frightened about facing the fact I was going to have to ask for what I wanted. Which, when it came to something deeply personal, I was utterly useless at. Thankfully, Gaines knew me, so I didn't have to explain it to him.

"Tell him how you feel. I heard Daddy talking to Weston and I believe he wants to be with you as much as you want it. Trust yourself."

"Look where that's gotten me in the past... do I need to mention putrid Peter? Or the lengthy list of other losers I've dated."

"Okay, you have a terrible track record of picking losers. Let me ask this, instead. Did you ever trust any of them enough to ask them to help you? Even with the small stuff?"

I met his stare, seeing exactly what he was getting at. "No."

"Did you hesitate to reach out to Weston on Monday?"

"No."

"Did you at any point consider he'd not answer because he might be busy with other stuff or refuse to come?"

"No!" I snapped, outraged at the idea Gaines would even suggest Weston would act that way.

He grinned widely. "There you go. You have the answers. Weston is different. You love him and I suspect the feeling is mutual. Now go wash your face so it doesn't look like you've been crying. I don't want Weston threatening to kick my butt. And then we are going to find our Daddies so you can suss out Weston on how he'll feel about you staying at his place every night. Forever." He got up and dragged me with him, giving me a hard hug. "Just don't forget me when you move out."

I clung on to him, burying my face in his neck, sniffing. "As if I could ever forget my best friend in the universe. Who else would let me use their stuff and not get cross when I make a mess?"

He pulled back to arm's length and wore a matching grin. "West-on."

"Daddy," I said at the same time.

"See, we both know this is right."

His smug expression remained as I washed and dried my face, then changed into a pair of jersey pants that had a cute matching purple top that declared "life is always better in grape" that were soft and cozy, to help settle my nerves at going down to face Weston.

"Stop fidgeting, you're making me nervous," Gaines whispered out the side of his mouth as we came down the stairs holding hands.

"I can't help it!" I whispered back.

"What's with the whispering?" Austin asked, surprising us both as Gaines jerked as hard as me when we turned to find Austin behind us, coming down the stairs.

"Where's my Daddy?" I demanded, feeling more than a little edgy.

Austin rested a reassuring hand on my shoulder when he came to a stop on the stair above us. "No need to worry. He's making dinner for us all in the kitchen."

"He is? He's staying for dinner," I asked stupidly.

Austin eyed me in that assessing way I'd seen him do before. "Is everything okay?"

"Yep." I didn't let go of Gaines' hand, needing moral support as I skipped down the last few stairs, not waiting for Austin to follow.

In the kitchen, the scent of frying meat and onions registered, but it was Weston, with his shirt sleeves rolled up and looking right at home that I focused on. Taking a deep breath, I said the first thing that came into my head. "Daddy, I don't want to sleep alone."

"You're hurting me," Gaines hissed, dragging my attention from the motionless man at the stove as Gaines tried to untangle our fingers.

"Sorry," I mumbled, releasing my vice-like grip on him, though my gaze was back on Weston, who'd turned to face me holding a fish slice in his hand.

"What are you saying, Pumpkin?"

His neutral expression and unwavering tone held no inflection at all, giving me very little to work with. "I... prefer sleeping with you."

"Don't you mean on me?" The corner of his eyes crinkled the way they did when he was making a joke.

I stepped closer to where he remained, for now working on forgetting we had an audience. "Well, yes, that too."

"I love it too. So what are you suggesting we do about it?"

Heart hurling down the hill like I'd attached skies to it, I held his gaze, unaware of the begging eyes I was giving him, or maybe I was. Nothing could hurt right then when this was about asking for something I really wanted. "If I said I wanted to sleep in your bed... every night... would that be okay?"

Down went the fish slice before he was scooping me up, hands under my bum, my hands buried in the hair at the base of his neck before he claimed my mouth in a toe curling kiss.

"Is that a yes, Daddy?" I asked breathlessly when he stopped and beamed at me in a way that made my heart continue on the slide down the hill towards my ribs.

"Yes." Another kiss. "Yes." The next kiss lasted longer, his mouth angling over mine, exploring the contours of lips. His tongue dipping in between my lips, gently exploring my mouth, groaning. "Yes," he murmured softly, a loving gaze holding mine.

"The meat's burning." Gaines' voice interrupted the moment and I found myself lowered to the ground.

Weston cursed and reached for the fish slice, going back to the stove where a smell of burning onion and meat was indeed emanating from.

"Is it salvageable?" Austin asked, his amusement clear in his tone.

"You could have watched the pan." Weston turned his attention to the other man when he chuckled aloud.

"You offered to cook."

The giggles bubbled up as I looked at Gaines. When he grinned and laughed, I couldn't stop myself from joining in.

"That's right, laugh it up." The fish slice got pointed at the three of us. "You'll all be eating the burned offerings!" His lips quivered, then Weston was laughing along with us. "If you can't beat them—"

"Join them," I finished, leaning on Gaines who wrapped his arms around my waist, peals of laughter filling the air.

This was the best day ever!

Chapter Twenty-One

Weston

Sorting out a tea party took way more effort and military precision with Matty climbing the walls with excitement. I'd set up the large table off the kitchen, which had the best view of the lake. The tableware was all new and everything matched, right down to the Beatrice Potter cutlery set I'd found when doing one of my Christmas present searches for Matty.

Although it was still a couple of weeks to Thanksgiving, I'd pulled out all the Christmas decorations I had for the boys to dress the tree I'd bought specially for Matty's playroom. I'd also bought gift sets, with beads, glitter, paper, pens, glue guns, and many other things so they could make decorations, too.

Had I gone a little mad and overboard? I had. I knew it. Austin and Warner knew it, but having Matty home, here with me, happy and bubbly, made it impossible not to want to keep him in that state. His happiness was vital to me. He'd hardly slept the night before with how excited he was to be hosting his first real play date.

"Daddy... Daddy... where are youuuuu?" he called from the direction of the bedroom. A short while ago, I'd sent him off to look for an outfit to wear to keep him occupied.

"In the kitchen," I said, grinning as I knew he'd already be heading to me, and I didn't need to shout. He'd been longer than I thought he would be, but then there were a lot of clothes to sort through. He'd brought two suitcases of his things with him on Wednesday evening, then refilled them on Thursday.

On Friday, with little space remaining in either the playroom or our bedroom, I'd vetoed the idea of collecting more things when Gaines informed me there was still half a closet and two sets of drawers remaining in Matty's bedroom. That didn't include the selection of stuffies that came in a large sack and were the first things Gaines had put into his playroom. I could see in the future I was going to have to consider remodeling the closet space in the apartment if he was going to fit everything in. Especially as I found it impossible to resist buying him things, too.

Clapping hands got me twisting to see Matty stood by the doorway, still wearing the pajamas I'd put on him when we got up. His preference was to sleep naked, not that I minded when it gave me access to all of him.

"That looks so pretty Daddy." He stepped closer, his hands going behind his back, almost like he was worried he'd mess up the table.

"I did it just how you said you wanted it."

His head tilted, and a hand came to tug on a curl. "I love it. Do you think Terrence and Gaines will love it, too?"

"They will." I ran a hand over the curls, cupping his cheek. "Did you pick out some clothes to wear?" With a large amount of clothes still in suitcases, I opted to let him choose something to wear today after seeing the mess.

A shyness came as he kicked at the floor with his bare foot. "I'm not sure which one to wear. Can Daddy pick for me?"

"Absolutely, let's go see what you have, then I can give you a shower and get you ready."

Back was the bubbly boy who couldn't stop chattering as we moved to the bedroom, where I chose a cute dungaree set in vibrant blue with geometric rainbow print over the bib and on the T-shirt.

On the bed, he'd laid out four binkies, all assorted colors. Up to now, he'd shown no preference on what he liked to suck on when he was Little, besides my thumb occasionally. For now, I didn't draw attention to them. In the bathroom, I stripped him and put on the shower, easily keeping out of the spray until Matty got playful, moving his hands to spray me with water. Curls plastered to his head, wearing a playful expression, I had to resist a driving urge to confess how I felt.

"Did you get Daddy wet?" I asked instead, listening to him giggle and squirm under my hands as I soaped his body.

"Nooo, Daddy got himself wet."

His regression was a pleasure to watch, and I grinned at him. "Isn't it your hands splashing Daddy's clothes?"

Eyes wide and full of mischief, he shook his head, spraying yet more water at me, so I gave up and stepped fully clothed under the spray, getting more giggles. He slid his arms around my waist and snuggled in. "I love you, Daddy."

My heart skipped several beats, stopping me from finding my voice. I squeezed him tightly to me and kissed the top of his head. "I love you too, Matty."

He lifted his head to look up, water glistening on his eyelashes like crystal drops. "Pumpkin, Daddy. I'm Daddy's Pumpkin."

"That you are." Clinging to him for a moment more, I let myself soak up the feelings of love coming from him before resuming washing him.

Several minutes later, my soaking clothes were in a heap on the bathroom floor after I worked fast to get dry and dressed to focus on Matty. I dried and dressed a squirming Matty, whose excitement was contagious. "Let Daddy get your socks on, please."

He wiggled the swinging legs at me from where I'd perched him on the end of the bed after dressing him in the top and dungarees. "Catch them Daddy. I've got dancing feet."

After a third attempt, he had one sock on and the pair of us were laughing when a buzzer alerted me to the arrival of our friends.

Matty was up and off the bed at a sprint, squealing as he ran out of the room with one bare foot. "Daddy, they're here!"

I shook my head, unable to stop grinning as I followed to see if he'd listened to my instruction never to just open the door without me present when he was in Little space.

He stood by the door, hopping up and down, not attempting to open it, his hands tucked behind his back. I'd quickly realized this was something he did to resist the temptation of doing something he was told not to.

His curls tumbled around his face, making him look like an angelic cherub. "Such a good boy for listening to Daddy. We can add another reward to your chart."

"Another reward, oh my." His hands clapped together as I reached for the lock.

The door was barely open before Matty dragged Terrence and Gaines off through the apartment. "Come see my bedroom."

Gone moments later, two coats lay on the hallway floor. I grinned at the two men standing in the doorway wearing matching looks of adoration, convinced I looked exactly the same and I couldn't find a thing wrong with it.

"Love looks good on you," Warner said as he came into the apartment, shrugging off a thick wool coat.

"It feels good." I offered a hand for the coat and waited for Austin to take off his. "He's a delight and I just want to say to you both while we're alone, thank you for the support over the Peter situation. I know that pulling out of a couple of jobs at the last minute couldn't have been easy to fix." It was something I'd not mentioned to Matty and had no intention of doing when I'd done it to ensure that I could watch out for him and help him settle into my home.

"What are friends for?" Warner ran a hand through his hair. "It was an easy fix with Saul looking for some extra work. Although I think it was to avoid doing any more training with you."

They came with me into the living space, having picked up their boys' coats, looking around with interest. "Fuck off, I'm not that bad!"

"You are. And don't forget the challenge we discussed," Austin pointed out, making me groan.

"I thought you'd forgotten about that with Warner interrupting us."

Warner glanced between us. "What did I miss?"

"A gym challenge and the loser has to wear something like the outfit Royal bought that was all bows and little else."

The groan from Warner sounded like he was in pain. "Nope, not happening. I'm not getting involved. You too are far too competitive for me, and I'd end up the loser in this."

I chuckled, taking the other two coats to hang them with the ones over the back of a chair, before turning to look at both men, hearing giggling coming from down the hallway. "I'm up for it. Warner can think up the challenge or I can and there's a gym in the building we can use."

"Fuck, no," Austin groaned and shook his head. "So not happening today!"

"Remember, this was your suggestion," I pointed out, trying hard not to laugh at Austin's worried expression.

"Yeah, that was before Saul told me how you beasted him in the gym."

I walked over to him, grinning cockily. "We can arrange a day, maybe get some of the other guys involved, make it a team thing. And I hope you're ready to lose."

Austin rolled his broad shoulders and gave me a hard stare that only made me laugh. "We'll see about that. And yeah, I'm sure some of the guys would be up for this as long as they haven't spoken to Saul!"

"Daddy... are you coming to play... pleaseeee?" Matty's loud request stopped the posturing and back were the three grinning fools mad for their boys.

"Coming," I called back, knowing he'd come looking for me if I didn't answer. "Looks like it's time to play." I winked at Austin. "Maybe this can be your warm up."

"Dick," he muttered good-naturedly, slapping me on the back. "I'll wipe that smug look off your face, see if I don't."

Chapter Twenty-Two

Matty

Nestled in the middle of my bed for nap time, with Gaines and Terrence squashed in too, I held my binkies in my hands. "Do you want one of mine, Terrence? Daddy says it's a nice thing to share." I offered, trying to stop his mouth from wobbling because he forgot his binkie.

He eyed my hand. "Did you suck on them?"

I giggled and pointed to the pink and yellow ones. "These two I like. I haven't used the blue or green ones."

"Can I have the green one?" he asked, a shy smile appearing when I nodded eagerly, and he reached out to take it.

"That means I'm left with the blue one." Gaines looked sad.

"Don't you like blue?" Terrence said hesitantly, his fingers curling around the green one he held, bringing it into his chest.

"I do, but I want my binkie." He glanced at the three men watching us, sitting on the rug surrounded by toys and stuffies. "Daddy, did you bring my binkie?"

Austin rose and nodded. "It's in my coat pocket. Give Daddy a second to get it."

Back to smiling, Gaines wriggled against me, snuggling into the fleece blankie that was bigger than the bed.

"Careful, you's poking me with your knee," I muttered, trying to get comfortable while squished in the middle. Not that I minded when my friends loved my bed and wanted to sleep in it with me.

More giggling ensued as Terrence rested his head on my shoulder, chewing on the binkie and making himself comfy. "I like your bed," he mumbled around his binkie.

His head lifted and he looked over at his Daddy, taking out the binkie. "Daddy, do you think I could get a new bed, one like this with the sparkle lights? Pleaseeee."

"See what you've started Wes," Warner replied, but didn't sound cross.

"Pleaseeee, Daddy," Terrence begged, his eyelashes moving weirdly as he stared at his Daddy.

A groan came before Warner's smile widened, making my tummy settle. "We'll go shopping next week, okay?"

"Tomorrow, Daddy?"

Warner shook his head. "Next week, I promise we'll go."

Terrence's body moved excitedly next to me and I whispered, "Why did you do the weird thing with your eyelashes?"

Gaines came closer and spoke in my ear. "'Cause it makes his Daddy say yes."

"Are you being cheeky?" Austin asked, bringing my attention to him as he held out the binkie that looked like it had koala ears. Gaines' favorite thing in the whole world.

Gaines' face went red, and he shook his head. "No, Daddy." He pushed the binkie into his mouth quickly.

"Daddy, are you gonna read us a story now?" I asked, wanting to make sure my friend didn't get into trouble. And though I preferred to lie on my Daddy when he read to me, it was nice to have my friends squished against me.

"Of course, what story do y'all want?"

I looked at the pile on the top of the chest and clapped my hands. "The Secret Lake." I looked at Gaines, then Terrence saying, "You're gonna love it. There's a missing dog and a boat that leads to a secret tunnel."

"A secret tunnel. Where does it go?" Terrence asked wide eyed.

"Pumpkin, don't spoil it for them," Daddy said.

I sighed loudly. "Okayyyy! But you have to hurry Daddy and start, otherwise they won't get to hear the best bits."

"Settle down and then I'll start." He got up and retrieved the book. Before he sat, he tucked us in and gave me a kiss. I was thinking he also wanted to have me on his tummy, so I reached up and rubbed his belly. "Next time, Daddy."

"Absolutely, Pumpkin." He lowered to the rug next to the bed and smiled at us. "Now, are we ready?"

I nestled in with my friends, popping the pink binkie between my lips. "We are," I mumbled around the binkie, feeling warm fuzzies in my belly when Daddy's deep voice started reading. I was a very lucky boy.

~/~/~/~

Nerves took hold as Weston pulled to a stop in the drive of my parents' home. I'd rung them to let them know I was bringing Weston with me this morning. I'd come to the conclusion quite some time ago that they differed from other parents. Gaines and his family had more than made up for their lack when it came to things like holidays and special occasions, like birthdays. My parents had never really got me, or me them. They loved me; I knew that. It was just that they were so involved in their own lives they often forgot to consider the impact of their decisions on me.

The Psychology books I'd read said it was why I struggled to ask for anything and I liked to be taken care of. With the memory of how wonderful the day before had been, I didn't care about the reasons I liked what I did. I'd found Weston being me, and I was perfectly fine with that.

"Are you sure you want me to come in with you?" Weston broke the silence in the car.

I huffed out a breath, unsure how to explain what he was going to witness with my parents' behavior. "It's not that I don't want you to come with me. I just don't know how to explain what they're like."

He took the hand I'd balled in my lap and stroked his fingers over the skin, warming it. "Then don't. Let's go in, do the introductions, and eat brunch. Then we can leave to go do something fun."

Fun. How was Weston going to compete with the amazing day before? After he'd read to us and we'd had nap time, we'd gotten up refreshed and spent the evening eating party food and making Christmas decorations. Some of the ones I'd made, I'd tucked into the bag sitting at my feet with the gifts I'd bought my parents, along with an expensive bottle of wine they enjoyed.

It was tradition for me to make Christmas tree decorations and it showed how much Weston listened when I talked about my past to make sure I could do it this year. My parents kept every one of my handmade decorations in beautiful little boxes, wrapped up and treasured. It was one of the many oddities that were my parents.

When Gaines and Terrence said they'd had the best day when they were leaving, I cried a little because I was so happy. Having my space and being able to invite my friends was special.

Exhausted, Weston had to put me to bed where I'd slept late, making me feel a little out of sorts when I'd no time to prepare Weston, which is why I sat without getting out of the car.

One glance up at the house and I nodded. "Can I claim one of my rewards?" I asked, needing something positive to keep me from spiraling into a nervous wreck.

"Of course you can." He kissed my cheek and then reached to unbuckle my seatbelt, leaning further over me to open the door. "Now let's go."

His firm Daddy tone was enough to get me out of the car without complaint. Bag in hand, I waited for him to come around the hood of the car, taking my hand to lead me up the steps.

I tried to view the large house as Weston might. It was imposing and big enough to easily house a family of ten. The garden surrounding the house was mostly lawn with a couple of trees and some bushes with no flowers. It was, as my parents explained, easy to maintain. That was their way. They liked things to be easy and run smoothly, something I'd learned at a very early age.

At the door, I knocked with the hand holding the bag, not wanting to let go of Weston before opening the door. Met with silence and the scent of baking, I walked down the long passageway, shoes clipping on the polished wooden floors. I led Weston towards the sunroom at the back of the house where my parents liked to eat Sunday brunch.

Our housekeeper, Debbie, appeared from the direction of the kitchen before we'd gotten halfway through the house. The rosy-cheeked woman with curly red hair that always looked a little wild, now peppered with streaks of gray, bustled towards us. She wasn't much taller than me but was so full of life she appeared bigger. "Matty, look at you all fresh as a bright daisy."

I kissed her powdered cheek, inhaling the scent of bread that she always smelled of. "A bright daisy, hey. I bet I couldn't compete with your smile and smell, both of which are like a little bit of heaven."

She laughed, a deep pink making her cheeks glow brighter. "Such a charmer." Her interest moved to Weston. "And who's this strapping man?"

"This is Weston, my boyfriend." I couldn't stop preening when she whistled and eyed him up and down.

"Why, you look like you caught yourself a keeper." She gave him a flirty wink before she bustled us towards where I could hear voices and the sound of operatic music. "Better not keep your parents waiting. You know how they'll fuss."

As we entered, I noted since my last visit they had changed the furniture in the sunroom. The seats around the table placed in the center of the room were now a floral design and matched the wall hangings and the curtains at the windows.

Dressed as if they were going out to dinner rather than an informal brunch with their son, I swallowed a sigh and plastered a smile on my face. "Mom, Dad, I'd like you to meet Weston, my boyfriend."

Dad rose, looking imposing, and held out his hand. An appraising gaze swept over Weston, not anywhere as friendly as Debbie's, who'd disappeared, no doubt back to the kitchen to get the tray of food and keep to my parents' schedule.

"Good to meet you. Call me Bruce and this is my wife Veronica," he said, while shaking Weston's hand.

"Nice to meet you, Bruce." Weston nodded at my mom as he let go of Dad's hand.

The jittery feeling increased as I went to Mom and kissed her cheek, getting a whiff of Dior. "You look lovely, Mom." I lifted the bag I held and offered it to her. "Just some gifts for you and Dad to pack for your vacation."

"How lovely," she murmured in a modulated tone, her gaze moving to Weston. "Sit now and tell me how you two met."

Sitting next to Weston, he placed a hand on my thigh under the table and squeezed before he answered. "In Milton Lee Olive park on a beautiful sunny day in August. Your son was out exploring the secret gardens of the city."

I only part listened to Weston as he continued to answer their questions, too busy watching for signs of how my parents felt about me bringing home a boyfriend for the first time. One who was decidedly older than me, something I'd not really given any thought to until I noted Weston had more silver hair than my father.

"Whereabouts do you live?" Dad asked, cutting into one of the freshly baked pastries Debbie had placed on the table along with an array of sandwiches, fruit and small savory tarts.

"I've an apartment on North Lake Shore Drive."

"It's got an amazing view of Lake Michigan," I replied enthusiastically. "The view from my bedroom is of the enormous Ferris wheel down on the boardwalk." It was difficult to keep my hand from slapping over my mouth for letting my lips take charge before my brain engaged when Mom's knife clattered to the plate, outwardly the only sign of concern.

"You've moved in together? So soon."

I gave an impassioned plea that they'd understand how important this man was to me. "Yes. And it's not so soon. It's November and we've been seeing each other since August." There was no way I was going to point out over two of those months it was only a Saturday date in the park. That, they would not understand. "I love Weston and want to be with him as much as possible."

"I see." Dad didn't sound like he did, and I hid my disappointment.

The hand on my thigh moved to take hold of mine and he placed our joined hands on the table. "I love your son very much. Him moving in is the right choice *for us*. You are both more than welcome to come for brunch, lunch or dinner when you return from your vacation. Check out where your son is living." As Weston spoke, he stroked his fingers over mine, keeping the anxiety from forming into a knot in my stomach.

There was a second of silence as my parents looked at each other, something passing between them. It was a language I'd never figured out.

"We'd like that very much." A smile lit my mom's eyes, making the tension in my shoulders release. "Wouldn't we Bruce?"

"We'll be back in the middle of January, just in time for your birthday on the 20th. We can visit then."

When Weston nodded, I let go of the breath that I'd held, waiting for Dad to answer. "Perfect. Tell me a little more about yourself, Weston."

Chapter Twenty-Three

Weston

Thanksgiving

There was such a stark difference between my family and Matty's, it was impossible not to notice. After the initial hiccup with Matty's parents discovering he had moved in with me, they'd warmed up. Or been a little more relaxed around me once they realized I was a stable guy who could more than take care of their son.

Although Matty had questioned me about what his dad had wanted to speak to me in private about, while his mom had taken him off to get the bag of gifts they'd bought for him, I'd kept most of it to myself. His dad was genuinely concerned about how he perceived his naïve son's welfare. Matty would, at some point, inherit a considerable sum of money and they were uneasy about him being taken advantage of. That I was the first man he'd brought home to meet them explained a lot. I hoped my reassurance that I'd sign any legal documentation to protect Matty had gone to easing their worries. It was a hard one to call.

Although that wasn't what had occupied my thoughts throughout brunch or after. When Matty had first declared his love for me, he'd been in Little space. In front of his parents, he'd blown me away by his declaration, not holding back his feelings. Two weeks on, he was getting bolder at expressing his feelings when he wasn't Little, and boy did it hit me in the heart when he did.

"Wes, get your head out of your backside and come help with cleanup," Pat, Mom's sister, called from the other side of the room, bringing me from my thoughts.

We'd arrived four hours earlier for Thanksgiving dinner, only to be surprised by the whole family. Mom had invited both my aunts and uncles, along with my cousins and their children. Half the time the adults talked over each other, laughing and joking, myself included, and this was what had started me thinking about the difference between Matty's family and my own.

I couldn't see his parents getting down on the floor to play with the children, like Matty was right now. Giggling and enjoying being free to play and not looking out of place because he was entertaining the children. Something he'd dived into with enthusiasm after his wide-eyed shock at seeing so many people in my childhood home.

Mom, who was superb at cook, hadn't lied about there being enough food to feed forty thousand as I eyed what remained on the kitchen counters, getting up to help with the cleanup.

A shoulder bump from my cousin David, and I turned, giving him an enquiring look. "Matty, he's a keeper with how he can keep the brats entertained without them falling out."

David was referring to his two children, Andrew, seven, and Grace, six. They fought over everything and were highly competitive with each other. "He loves kids." It was easier to say that than the truth.

"Great, then maybe you two would be interested in babysitting."

"Stop tapping up Wes for babysitting duties. You've already got enough willing victims," my aunt Rosemary said from the kitchen sink, where she was up to her elbow in soap suds.

David's deep laughter drowned out the kids' giggles and shouts. "There are never too many in my book. Gotta cover all my bases, Mom."

"Don't you always," I answered, knowing he'd been no different, even as a child.

The conversation continued as I dried the dishes and David put them away. I kept my eye on Matty, who currently sat surrounded by four children, all vying for his attention as he showed them how to make finger puppets from the large bag of bits Mom kept for times like this.

"Who's ready for dessert?" Mom called out, getting squeals and shouts, the loudest coming from Matty, who scrambled up as fast as the others.

He glowed, literally. The large Christmas tree tucked in the corner full of twinkling lights couldn't compete with him.

He came and tucked himself into my body, grinning at me as I ran a hand over his T-shirt to the band of his jeans. "You looked like you were having fun."

"I was… Weston."

My lips twitched at how he'd deliberately taken his time to say my name. I kissed his forehead, getting several oohs and ah's from the females in the room. "Give over, guys."

Rosemary sniffed and wiped the corner of her eyes. "You were right Nina, they are adorable together."

"Mom!" I chastised, getting a shrug in response with a cheeky grin.

"It's true."

"It'll be wedding bells next, Nina, and then you'll need to buy a new outfit," Pat said, laughing.

What I didn't expect was Matty's giggles as he pushed a hand into the back pocket of my jeans and squeezed my ass.

"Didn't someone say dessert?" I muttered, trying to figure out how I felt about marrying the man who fit me perfectly.

I let myself get distracted by serving up dessert, then clearing up, before those with children decided it was getting late and time to leave.

Thirty minutes later, I stood on the doorstep giving Mom a hug. "Thanks for today… I know it must have been hard."

"No. Not like I thought it would be. You all helped and I'm sure he was watching over us, happy we were all moving on and living life." She glanced at Matty, who was saying goodbye to Grace and Andrew at the curb. "He helped, too." She cupped my cheeks and held my stare. "He's a special young man. One who fits you. Someone like that, you don't let go of."

I grinned at the not-so-subtle hint. "You taking pointers off Aunt Rosemary?"

"She takes them from me. And think about it. These last few years, life has taught me waiting for the right moment, we miss the moments that are happening right now. It's too late to go back. Live for now, Weston. You deserve that, as does that special man." She kissed my forehead and let go of my face, her eyes glistening with tears. "Now go take your young man home before he gets dragged into David's car by the kids."

A ball of emotion lodged in my throat and my nod was a little jerky when she stepped back inside the doorway out of the wind. "Don't forget our lunch date on Sunday, Matty," she called out. "You need to show me how to make those parmesan potatoes you made for today."

After another round of goodbyes and discussion for the Christmas holidays, we were in my car on the way home.

"Is it always a riot of noise like that when you all get together?"

The way the words came out a little slurred suggested he was going to fall asleep any second. "It's been a while since we've all been together like that. But yeah, it can get pretty loud. And I'm sorry, Mom didn't warn me, otherwise I'd have said something about it." I imagined Thanksgiving for him up to now with a full on family was an uncommon and novel experience.

"I loved it," he murmured, his eyes already closing when I glanced over at him.

"Sleep. Daddy will wake you when we get home."

There was a quiet murmur, which I surmised was an 'okay', before he shoved a thumb between his lips and his head lolled towards the window.

Lights lit up the interior of the car as I drove down busy roads, my mind going over what Mom had said. Marriage. The concept was nowhere as scary as it could be when it came with thoughts of Matty being my husband. My forever partner.

Could anyone put a number on the length of time that was appropriate to know someone before considering a lifelong commitment? For me, it would be that. I'd never consider taking this step lightly, and I suspected Matty would be the same.

Time. How much of it did one need to consider that love was real, deep and everlasting?

I shook my head at how no one could answer that. Love was individual and what for some might take years, for others could be from the first meeting. Did I love Matty? Yes, with every fiber of my body. These last couple of weeks had proven that to me repeatedly. He was a joy to be with; playful, kind, loving, and everything I could want in a man.

As I let those feelings settle, others rose at how I'd feel if I lost out on the opportunity to show him daily how much he means to me. A sob choked me and I blinked furiously, getting just a little more understanding of how Mom must feel without Dad. Her words on replay, I pulled into the underground garage to park up.

Matty never moved as I opened the door and went around to get him out of the car. He mumbled a complaint, but didn't open his eyes as I shook him gently.

Giving in a moment later, releasing his seatbelt, I scooped him up in my arms, using my backside to shut the door. He pushed his head into my neck and sighed. "Love you, Daddy."

"I love you too, Matty," I whispered, carrying him to the lift, my thoughts right back to what I should do next.

Chapter Twenty-Four

Matty

Christmas Eve

The suction on my cock curled my toes into the mattress as I struggled to keep still. Weston had promised me a reward if I didn't move or come without his permission. When I'd agreed, I'd not considered he'd play dirty. The three lubed fingers he thrust into my ass with ease proved my point. He had taken so long to stretch me I could barely keep any part of me motionless. I'd tried using a complicated design problem to distract myself, only it wasn't working any longer.

"I need to move, Daddy." My cock throbbed, as did my balls with how he added pressure to them, preventing me from coming.

I groaned in complaint when his mouth left my cock. Positioned as I was, I couldn't see his face, but I could tell when he spoke he was grinning. "Then move, but remember, you won't get my reward."

"Not fair," I moaned when his tongue ran over the head of my cock, and he blew on the sensitive skin, making me shiver.

"Now what kind of Daddy would I be if I didn't make my Pumpkin earn his reward? I promise it will be worth it."

"Then can we hurry Daddy... please..." I panted, moaned and cried out, unable to finish speaking when the fingers in my ass rubbed at my prostate, sending my overheated system into combust mode with the added pressure to the slit of my cock as he pushed the tip of his tongue in.

My thigh quivered with the need to thrust up and push down at the same time, to ride the fingers working to steal my ability to remain still and do as he wanted. But Weston's rewards were so good, I really wanted to know what it was he had planned.

When he eased his fingers out of my ass, I groaned anew, feeling empty, then I was rolling until Weston was beneath me and I was straddling his thighs, his aroused, lube covered cock sitting right under my balls. I rocked over the hard flesh, stifling my moan when he arched his eyebrows at me. "I was steadying myself, Daddy."

"Is that so?"

I nodded, holding my lower body still when his cock bucked against me.

"Lift your bottom and lean over Daddy's chest," he growled, and I moved as fast as Sonic the Hedgehog when I got what was going to happen next.

"So eager for Daddy's cock." His chuckle was dark and dirty as he reached between us and lifted his cock up. He wasn't wrong. "Remember, no coming until Daddy says."

As if I needed reminding!

He pushed the head of his cock against the loosened muscle of my ass. The snick of the rim clasping the head of his cock as he sank in got me panting heavily while attempting to hold my position. My cock bobbed as the pressure in my backside increased when Weston used his free hand to guide me down on his shaft.

My mouth became dry by the time I settled on him fully. His thick girth made me feel him everywhere, stretching and burning.

"Hold on," he gritted out, his hands going to my hips. He steadied me, waiting for my signal that I was okay.

The tightness of his jaw and dark hue of color over his cheeks revealed he was in no better condition than me with the need to come. Flattening my hands on his chest, I held his glittering gaze as I squeezed the throbbing length in my ass, encouraging him to move. He rocked, gently at first.

My cock bobbed between us as he upped the pace, stroking deeper. My eyes rolled when he hit just the right spot every time he rolled his hips up. Not counting it as moving, I squeezed his cock once more. The animalistic sound that tore from his throat sent shivers of desire through me. He came up, pushing all the way inside me, trapping my cock against his stomach while he claimed my mouth in a punishing kiss.

Out of control, I attacked him, my teeth hitting his as the hour of teasing he'd done proved to be my undoing. Hands clawing at his back, I rocked my hips, ass clasping hard, wanting him to lose it too.

We tumbled over the bed, a tangle of limbs, his mouth not releasing mine. He crowded over me, pushing back in. His hips slapped against mine as I wrapped my legs around him and held on. The sweat coating his skin aided the slick drive of my cock over his rippling muscles.

Pre-cum smeared his skin as he sped up and I ripped my mouth from his, gasping, "Can... I... come... Daddy?" The latter was only a strangled moan.

"Come for Daddy," he demanded in a harsh growl before his mouth captured mine.

I cried out into his mouth as my body let go, cum splattering between us when I felt the warmth of his cum deep in my ass.

Sweaty, chest heaving, I lay in the tangle of sheets trying to catch my breath when, minutes later, Weston rolled off to the side, leaving a hand on my sticky stomach next to my spent cock.

"Did... I... earn... my reward?" I twisted my neck to look at the man who was also struggling to catch his breath.

He peeled one eye open and looked at me, wearing a satisfied expression that never failed to make me happy. His lips formed into a cheeky grin that got my pulse jumping around. "Yes."

The exhaustion forgotten, I sat up eagerly. "What is it? Can I have it now?"

His laughter came in short bursts as he rolled off the bed and rose. The light coming through the windows highlighted every glorious inch of him and I forgot myself for a moment. "Where are you going?" Our plans for Christmas Eve were a movie marathon. All my choices.

"Where are we going?" He held out his hand. "We need to shower and get dressed."

I crossed my arms over my chest for good measure, making it obvious I wasn't taking his hand. "We're having a movie marathon. Why do I need to get dressed?" I pouted.

"That was before you were so good at winning a reward."

Off the bed in a second, I ran past him to the bathroom, hearing the sounds of his laughter.

Weston teased and tormented me with a guessing game on what the reward might be as we showered, dried and got dressed in warm clothes, making me suspicious he'd planned something before he'd offered me a reward. "What are you planning, Daddy?"

He tweaked my nose, then guided me into the kitchen. "You'll have to wait and see."

As we'd gone back to bed after breakfast, it surprised me when we went into the kitchen. At the large standing cupboard, in which he stored big items that he didn't seem to use, he retrieved a bulging pack. The kind professional hikers use.

My eyes narrowed on the bag, trying to guess what could be inside. It was big and looked heavy as he carried it to where he'd slung our winter coats the night before, after coming back from his mom's for dinner. She was spending Christmas with Rosemary and her family. We'd gotten an invitation, which Weston had declined, stating as it was our first Christmas together, he wanted to spend it alone with me. Something I was excited about with the enormous Christmas tree next to the window and a stack of gifts beneath.

It was a difficult talk with Gaines about my plans as this was the first time in more than a decade we wouldn't be spending Christmas day together. We had a cry and then decided to have a sleepover on Boxing day at his house, with me and Weston sleeping in my bedroom. It was still my room, Gaines assured me it always would be. It was nice to know, though I'd never been more confident I wouldn't need it unless it was for sleepovers. Weston loved me and he expressed that love daily. His one annoying trait, I'd discovered, was that he was fantastic at keeping secrets!

"Daddy, you're up to something," I stated as he helped me into my thick coat, pulling out my hat and gloves from the pocket, making me suspect wherever we were going, we were walking. He tucked my curls under the brim of the woolen hat. I'd grown them out, loving how Weston liked to stroke them when he read to me.

He dressed in similar clothes to me, ready for the cold, then slung the pack over his back to take my gloved hand. "We're ready."

"For what?"

He was having fun. I could tell by how pleased he looked with himself. "Wait and see."

He locked up and we headed down in the empty elevator to the ground floor. Two men were at the reception talking. Weston waved a greeting but kept going out the front of the building. The sky was bright, but the wind was cold against my cheeks as Weston guided me down the street toward the lake.

A minute later, he crossed over the street and took a turn, making me grin. "Are we going to our secret park?"

"We are."

I leaned back to look at the pack he wore, considering what could be inside with this latest information. "Are we going to have a winter picnic in the park?" The idea, despite the cold, was appealing with how bright it was and after expelling so much energy in the bedroom, I was getting hungry.

"See, you are back to being a good guesser."

I danced at the side of him, pulling on his hand, trying to get him to go faster so I could see what he'd packed for our Christmas Eve picnic in the park.

He guided us to the spot where we'd first met. "When I planned this, I asked Dad to make sure the weather Gods were kind to us." As he spoke, he took off the pack, lowered it to the ground with shaking hands and unzipped the top, revealing a blanket.

My gaze moved from the pack to him and back to the hands that were clearly trembling as he tugged out the blanket and laid it on the ground. "That day I ran through the park in August, I did not know it would change my life."

My belly quivered with nerves as next came several small plastic tubs, two plastic cups and a bottle of expensive champagne my parents liked.

"Meeting you was like coming out of a barren desert I'd been trapped in for months, suddenly finding myself in an oasis with an abundance of beauty." He turned, kneeling down on one knee, a small velvet box held in his hand.

A sob caught in my throat. "Weston..." I sniffed and dashed a hand at the stray tear that had the nerve to run down my cheek and obscure the man in front of me.

His expression was serious and my heart refused to beat. "I couldn't imagine my life without you. Will you marry me?"

Unaware I'd moved, I found my face buried in Weston's neck, sobbing like a baby. Big wracking sobs.

Enfolded in his arms, he sat me on his raised knee. The scent of his aftershave came with each breath I sucked in. "It's okay, Pumpkin. Daddy's got you."

"I know," I sobbed, unable to stop them with all the emotions clashing together at the enormity of the situation.

"Breathe for me." A hand rubbed up the back of my padded coat. "Come on, breathe." He continued to talk to me, using a soothing tone.

Gathering myself, I scrubbed my hands over my wet, chilly face and looked down to see where the velvet box had gone. An undignified sniff later, I asked, "Can I see it?"

"The ring?"

I nodded and found him using one arm to keep me steady as he reached to the ground and picked up the box. A box he'd drop to hold me and keep me safe first, it showed what kind of man he was at his core. I was more important than any object, regardless of what it was.

His thumb flipped the lid back and my mouth opened, but no words came out. There, nestled in the black velvet, was a band about a quarter inch wide full of glittering stones. I reached out and traced a fingertip over the stones.

"I couldn't pick one stone, so the jeweler suggested using a collection. It reminded me of you. A rainbow in a storm."

The tears were ready to start again and I swallowed twice before I moved my attention to Weston. "Ask me again. I promise not to spoil it this time."

His smile, god it was beautiful.

"Matty, Pumpkin, will you marry me?"

With difficulty I inhaled and then exhaled, plucking out the ring, clutching it in my hand, then held it out to Weston. "Put it on me, but only if you promise never to take it off."

His laughter rumbled out as he dropped the empty box and took the ring, slipping it on my ring finger. It fit perfectly.

He kissed me softly. "This is why I love you. You never do the expected."

"The expected is boring." I kissed him hard on the mouth, enjoying his swift intake of breath, before I turned my attention to the blanket. "So what's my reward?"

"Me," he exclaimed through more laughter.

I rested my head on his shaking shoulder, looking out at the park where it had all started. "Daddy, now that's a reward!"

Epilogue

Weston

Challenge Time

It had taken a little longer to get everyone together for the physical challenge than expected. Warner was going to be the judge, as he'd been adamant he wasn't going to join in. As it was the second of January, the gym in my building was empty at this time of the morning. Which was a good thing when I eyed the twelve intimidating men roaming around, preparing in little more than shorts for what was coming. The group of men, most of whom I'd met, had ignored Saul's warning. Although I'd noticed he was here too.

I kept the grin to myself, my competitive spirit coming to the fore at what I'd organized with Warner. Whoever got the lowest score out of 200 repetitions over four exercises would have to do the forfeit, and that would happen tonight. Austin had arranged a work's meal for this evening, where one of us would wear the skimpy bow dress Warner had sourced for the occasion. It would be the ultimate humiliation for someone, but it wasn't going to be me.

Joseph, Cody, Harvey, Yusuf, Luke, Jake, Aiden, Lewis, Matthew, Saul, Aaron, and Austin came over when Warner called, "As everyone is here, shall we get started?"

I closed the door leading into the gym behind a giggly Matty, Gaines and Terrence. They weren't the only men who'd come to support their boyfriends. Several other men sat on mats on the far side of the room, some of whom I'd met and knew they were in relationships with Saul, Cody, Harvey and Aiden.

Matty came up on his tiptoes and puckered up. I gave him a kiss and heard both Gaines and Terrence groan. Gaines had spent all day boxing day admiring Matty's engagement ring. I was sure it wouldn't be long before he had one of his own, by how Austin had stared at his boy.

"Come on, we need to find a good seat so we can watch as my Daddy trounce yours," Gaines boasted.

Matty spun to look at his friend, hands on hips. "My Daddy is a beast, you wait and see. He's going to make your Daddy cry."

"Boys, sportsmanship applies to the support teams, too," Warner pointed out, slipping an arm around Terrence's shoulder.

"You're only saying that 'cause you was a coward," Matty declared, making everyone laugh except Warner and Terrence.

"My Daddy is not a coward. He'll show your Daddy."

"Terrence... he's goading you," Warner spluttered.

"I know, but you'll show him, won't you?" his tone pleading, along with his eyes as he stared up at Warner.

I swallowed my chuckle when I saw the moment he caved. "Looks like we need a new referee."

"I'll do it," a dark-haired man said, sitting next to Will, Cody's boyfriend. The similarities between them suggested they were brothers. "I'm not dating anyone here, so I'll be impartial." He sounded sad about that when I saw him cast a longing glance in Lewis's direction.

"Fine," Warner muttered crossly. "I'll need a pair of shorts."

"My gym bag is in the locker room," I said. "You'll find a clean pair in there that should fit you."

"Thanks!"

I couldn't stop the laughter at how he sounded anything but grateful, though Terrence was beaming.

I clapped my hands together. "Make sure you all warm those muscles."

To the dark-haired man, I lifted a hand and beckoned him to me. I tugged out my cell phone from my shorts pocket and clicked through my apps, finding the routine we were about to do. "What's your name?" I asked, smiling down at the very short guy.

"Arlo."

"Okay, Arlo, this is what everyone is going to be doing. We will time each section. Everyone needs to complete fifty repetitions in the designated one minute. We'll go in pairs, so you might want Will to help. Though make sure he doesn't get to count for Cody to keep it fair."

His gaze never left the screen as he watched the video of the guy doing the routine. "You're gonna do those moves fifty times in a minute?" he questioned, sounding doubtful.

"We're sure as hell going to try." The men in the room were all experienced in hand to hand combat and that required a good level of fitness, so I didn't see it as an enormous challenge for any of them. The key was stamina and focus.

When Warner returned, Arlo paired everyone up. With the addition of Warner to the numbers, there were seven pairs. I got paired with Austin, who groaned in complaint. "Why do I get Wes?"

"'Cause this was your idea, that's why!" Warner snapped, still pissed it would seem.

"Settle down," Arlo said, with enough force to surprise everyone into silence. "Okay, first up is Weston and Austin. Weston, can you show the move to everyone? You are required to do fifty in one minute. You'll be ranked by the number you successfully complete. Will and I will keep a record on our phones. Our decision is final on the count and that will decide who the loser is and who gets to wear the pretty dress." He wore a gleeful expression. One he directed at Lewis, making me wonder if there was something going on between them.

Austin retrieved the bag with the dress that was only a few strategically placed bows over nipples, ass and, for a guy, his cock. He held up the red satin 'dress' and grinned at the groaning group. "This is what you are fighting to avoid wearing tonight."

At the laughter, I got down on the floor, doing a few more stretches. I'd warmed up in my apartment before coming down. "The move is as follows. Legs up off the ground while leaning back as far as you can go. Twist right, then left hands together going towards the floor but not quite touching. You'll do two upper body twists, then bring your feet up and touch the toes of your sneaker with the opposite hand. We do that twice, too. Only your ass touches the ground during that minute, got it?" There were grunts as I showed them what they had to do.

"I've got the stopwatch on my cell phone set. Are you ready?" Arlo stood to my left and Will to Austin's right.

"Yep."

"Yes, as I'll ever be," Austin said, giving me a hard stare.

"On three. One, two, three."

Concentrating on keeping my moves fluid, I blocked out the catcalls. Breathing through my nose, I stared at Matty, who moved into my line of sight wearing a shit-eating grin. He was all the motivation I needed.

"Time," Arlo called out.

Sweat slid down the center of my back as I got up and cricked my neck from side to side, stretching my arms over my head to loosen my stomach muscles.

"Wow! Weston got fifty-three and Austin you got forty-nine," Will said, his finger tapping at the screen on his cell phone.

I winked at Matty and gave a little bow to Austin, winding him up.

By the end of the first round, I tied with Harvey and Lewis was at the bottom with forty-two. "Next, is a press up and your start position is on your elbows. You need to reach forward and tap the floor, one hand at a time, staying on your elbows. Doing this twice. Then come up to side plank, arm stretching to the sky and back then under your body, twice, before starting again."

This got more groans as I showed what was required.

Saul shook his head, groaning. "I bet you devised this damn routine."

"Nope, this one isn't mine. It's one from the calisthenic academy." The time restriction and number required to make it harder, that was all me. I didn't say that part, though Warner was fully aware of it.

"Remind me never to agree to shit like this again," Harvey moaned as he got down on the floor, this time him and Lewis going first.

I was up second to last, and Matty was back in position. Only this time, it was harder to focus on him with what I needed to do. Sweating, heart racing and my limbs trembling, I stopped when Arlo called time.

"Shit, you really are a beast. I think we should all give up now," said Cody.

"How did I do?" I asked, wiping the sweat off my face with the towel Matty handed me.

"Fifty-one," Matty answered before Arlo could, but he nodded in agreement.

In the lead, with Harvey right behind me, I grinned widely at everyone.

"Who thought this was a good idea?" Saul asked, looking directly at Austin, who shrugged, while slinging his towel around his neck to catch the sweat dripping from his hair.

"What's next?" Harvey asked. "You haven't won yet."

Back on the ground resting on my elbows, I stretched my legs out behind me and started running on the spot, then did an elbow press up to a full press-up while still running.

"Jeez, we're fucking screwed."

I didn't see who said that, but the laughter got stuck in my throat as I stopped to take a breath.

At the end of that round, Jake had slipped to the bottom and Warner wasn't far behind him. Terrence was looking pale faced and sat cuddling Gaines. The other men had gathered closer and were now shouting encouragement at all of us.

I spotted two men with tented jeans, right along with Matty. Appearing so focused on what was happening, he hadn't noticed his obvious reaction.

Arlo waved his hand in the air, attracting everyone's attention. "This is the last challenge so those at the bottom will go first. That's Jake and Lewis."

"Let's see the last humiliation." Lewis wore a defeated look.

I didn't explain this time, as it was easily replicated. I stood, then bent forward, creeping along the floor until fully stretched out, doing a full body press-up with extended arms, then hand walked back to standing.

"I damn well knew it," Lewis groaned, rubbing at his face. "Those things suck."

I had to agree; they were my least favorite.

Once we'd started, the shouts and jeers increased to deafening levels as everyone encouraged each other to do their best. This was what I loved about the collective group that Warner and Austin had hired. They were all about supporting each other, despite being competitive.

At the top of the leaderboard, I went last with Harvey. There were four points between us. Matty stood directly in front of me and kept his engagement ring right in my eyeline as he mouthed, "reward."

Getting his drift and a little energy boost at thoughts of what came after we'd finished, I winked at him. I got into position, took a deep breath, and cleared my mind.

"One, two, three."

There wasn't a muscle group that wasn't burning as I worked at a speed that this exercise wasn't supposed to be at. Sweat made my eyes sting as it slid down my face as I strained to get back up, my stomach muscles cramping at the effort.

"Time," Arlo called, and I dropped to the floor, resting my head on the back of my hands, dragging in deep breaths.

"My Daddy won." Matty was clearly gloating as his sneakered feet danced close to where my face was resting.

"Who's wearing the dress?" I asked, rolling onto my back and sitting up, having got my breath back.

From the look on Lewis's face, I didn't need to guess. Arlo picked up the bag and offered it to him. The smile that appeared on Arlo's face revealed two dimples but Lewis didn't take the bag. Instead, he stood staring at Arlo like he'd never seen him before.

Cheers and jokes flowed around me as I got up and found myself catching Matty as he jumped at me—a very aroused Matty—who wrapped his legs around my middle as I cupped his backside. "Daddy, you need a shower."

That was an understatement with how I felt like I'd just stepped out of the shower, I was so wet.

It didn't stop him from getting closer and whispering in my ear, "And it's my turn to help."

No further encouragement needed, I headed to the doors, waving a hand in the air. "See you guys later. I'm going for a shower."

"Yeah, right, a shower," Austin shouted after me, laughing.

I raised my middle finger, giving him the bird as I kept going when Matty licked up the side of my neck, groaning.

"Daddy's sweaty, Pumpkin."

His giggles brushed over my damp skin. "I know, you taste salty... I wonder if you taste salty everywhere?"

My knees hadn't let me down through all the strenuous exercise, but what Matty was implying made my legs weak. "Let's go find out."

His tongue ran back up my throat. "Lets, Daddy."

About the Author

Eccentric cake lover who has a passion for words of all kinds. I'm Jayne or JP, I live in the Isle of Man. A tiny place in the Irish sea where all the magic happens. I'm a confessed bookaholic and if I'm not writing I love to snuggle with a book or two...if you catch my drift.

If you're interested in keeping up to date, then I've a few places you can do that, and they're listed below. My website is where you'll find all the different Me's there are, LOL. As I travel this path into the future,

I'm going to be writing in different genres so to stop there being any confusion I'll be writing under different pen names.

If you would like to give me any feedback or just have any questions, go ahead and friend me on Facebook, and I would be happy to answer anything. I hope you enjoyed this book and if you would also like to leave a review, then I would love to read your thoughts. Even if you just want to rate it, I'll be grateful

Thank you for being a part of my dream.

Newsletter Sign up
Goodreads
Tumblr
Bookbub
Instagram
Twitter
Facebook
Website address
Facebook Author page
JP Manx Minx's
Patreon

Other Books By the Author

Standalone

When Fake Changed Everything

Christmas beyond Christmas

The Elves and the Bondage Daddy (Grim and Sinister Delights Book 5)

Agrippa My Heart

His Boy to Tease

Headshot

A Brat For Kinkmas

A Little Christmas: Terrence

Hanging With Daddy

Music & Dreams: Rocktoberfest

A Sucker for Christmas

Series

Assassins To Order With Lisa Oliver

Marvin – Marvin and Ajani

Ben – Ben, Teilo & Nico

Duron – Duron & Beaumont

Conrad – Conrad & Kylo

Dancing with the Devil – Wyatt & James

Tangled Tentacles Series with Lisa Oliver

Alexi #1

Victor #2

Todd #3

Markov # 4

Kelvin # 5

Little Paws Haven Series

Little Treasure he Hides

The Potters Creek Series

A Christmas Wish (book one)

The App Series

The App: Daddy kink (book one)

The App: Littles (book two)

The App: Puppy play (book three)
The Flamingo Bar Series
Always More (book one)
The Little Side of Me (book two)
3 Is the Magic Number (book three)

La Trattoria Di Amore Series
Puzzle Pieces (book one)
Dominated but not Subdued (book two)
Made to Submit

The Playroom Series
Mine, Body and Soul: Part One
Mine, Body and Soul: Part Two
Mine, Body and Soul: Part Three
Ferron's Journey: Damaged Part One (book four)
Ferron's Journey: Hidden Part Two (book five)
Ferron's Journey: Revelation Part Three (book six)
Mine, Body and Soul Trilogy
Ferron's Journey Trilogy
Spinoff Love's Heart Print

Dark River Stone Collective Series
The Light Beneath the Dark (Book One)
When Darkness Turns to Light (Book Two)
Running From Darkness (Book Three)

The Billionaire Playground Series
Property of a Billionaire (Book one)
Reluctant Billionaire (Book two)

Billionaire's Muse (Book three)

Heart Stones Series

Blood King

Enchanted Ink Series

Magic, Demons and the Hunter

The Manx Cat Guardians Series Where it all Began: Origins (Book 1)
Seeing Beyond the Scars (Book 2)
Destiny Collides Past and Present (Book 3)
Searching for a Soul to Love (Book 4)
The 12 Disasters of Christmas (Book 5)
Laws of Attraction (Book 6)
The Teacher's Boy (Book 7)
Boxset

Audio Books
Mine, Body and Soul, Part One: The Playroom Series
Mine, Body and Soul, Part Two: The Playroom Series
Mine, Body and Soul, Part Three: The Playroom Series
Daddy Kink: The App (book one)
Always More: The Flamingo Bar (book one)
When Fake Changed Everything
Ferron's Journey: Damaged Part One
Ferron's Journey: Hidden Part Two

Ferron's Journey: Revelation Part Three

Romance books in a mixed series of M/F and M/M by the Author under a different pen name Jayne Paton

Smith's Corner
Delilah & Dallas (book one)
Layla & Levi (Book two)
Ash & Alora (Book three)
Fox & Faith (book four)
Storm & Stone (book five)
Hunter & Holden (book six)

Crime and Thrillers by the Author under a different pen name J Paton

Headspace
Chozen: Dark MM Crime Drama (Headspace Book 1)
Chozen: Dark MM Crime Drama (Headspace Book 2)